"I have a daughter."

Jessica's breath caught in her throat, and she had to replay the words to process them completely.

A daughter.

Jessica's eyes started to tingle, and she prayed he'd believe the tears were from the cold. "I'm very happy for you," she said. Then she swallowed, cleared her throat and said exactly what she hadn't planned to say to him tonight. "I have a son."

The shock on his face matched hers.

"You have a son?"

Jess smiled and nodded, her cheeks pressing upward and causing that tiny river of tears to spill over. Again, she prayed he thought it was from the cold.

They both stood there for a moment, a bounty of words and explanations tumbling through her thoughts but none spoken.

Then she moved away from Chad Martin, away from the only man she'd ever loved and away from the man whose eyes were identical to the ones she'd see when she returned home…to his son.

RENEE ANDREWS

spends a lot of time in the gym. No, she isn't working out. She and her husband, a former all-American gymnast, own an all-star cheerleading gym. She is thankful the talented kids there don't have a problem when she brings her laptop and writes while they sweat. When she isn't writing, she's typically traveling with her husband, bragging about their two sons or spoiling their bulldog. Write to her at Renee@ReneeAndrews.com or visit her website at www.reneeandrews.com.

Her Valentine Family

Renee Andrews

Published by Steeple Hill Books™

STEEPLE HILL BOOKS

ISBN-13: 978-0-373-87653-2

HER VALENTINE FAMILY

This edition published by arrangement with Steeple Hill Books.

www.SteepleHill.com

Printed in U.S.A.

As the heavens are higher than the earth,
so are my ways higher than your ways
and my thoughts than your thoughts.
—*Isaiah* 55:9

This novel is dedicated to my parents,
James and Jolaine Bowers.
God blessed me with you.

ACKNOWLEDGMENT

Special thanks to Dr. Patrick Whitlock
for his patience in answering all of my
medical questions. All mistakes are mine.

Chapter One

Chad Martin left the Math and Science building at Stockville Community College after his last class Thursday evening mentally reviewing the semester's syllabus, which he'd spent the majority of class time explaining to the students. Sure, he crammed a ton in the Advanced Biology course, but he wanted them, or rather their parents, to get their money's worth. And he wanted to prove to the university that he could handle higher level courses in spite of his youth, show them that he could make the work challenging for the students but also entice them to enjoy the learning process. No, he hadn't planned on being a teacher, but if teaching was what he was doing, he wanted to do a good job.

He was so engrossed in calculating what he could cover the first week that he nearly missed the movement to his right, the slight shadow crossing the quad at an angle and heading toward the parking lot. The woman wore a midlength dark coat cinched tight around her waist and jeans. Her hair bounced against her shoulders as she moved, and her arms cradled several books to her chest. Small puffs of wispy smoke escaped her mouth as her warm breath hit the crisp January air. Northern Alabama wasn't as cold as most of the country at this time of year, but it was cold enough to cause her to huddle into herself as she briskly walked.

It was dark, but the campus lighting cast yellow ovals at sporadic intervals on the quad, and Chad stayed where he was, waiting for her to step inside the next patch of light. There was something so familiar about the way she moved, and he wondered whether he was doing it again—expecting to see Jessica one more time. For six years, he'd occasionally glimpsed someone who looked like her, walked like her, laughed like her. And each and every time, when he garnered the courage to approach the woman in question, he would see that his eyes, his ears had played tricks on him again. Jessica Bowman had walked out of his world six years ago, and he was a fool to think she'd suddenly burst back in.

But something about this woman…

Finally, she stepped completely into the circle of light. Then she paused her pace, flipped open the top book in her arms and then ran a hand in her purse and withdrew a pen. She scribbled something on the page, nodded and then put the pen away.

And he knew. This wasn't merely another woman who resembled Jessica. After practically every class in high school, when they'd walk to the lockers, her mind would churn over everything that happened in the classroom, and she'd inadvertently remember some little tidbit that the teacher had said, something to do with her homework or any other thing that she didn't want to forget later. After she made the notation, she'd nod in satisfaction and continue down the hall, the same way this woman did, as she plunked her pen back in her purse and started to walk again.

Thankfully, the light covered her for long enough that Chad, now moving toward her, saw her completely. Her hair was shorter than it'd been back then but still long enough to suit her youth, with honey strands accenting the shiny chocolate hue. What would she be now, twenty-two? No, twenty-three. Have mercy, it'd been a long time.

A pale pink scarf circled her neck, its fuzzy length trailing down her back and the fringed trim dangling below the edge of her coat. Her jeans were cuffed, he now noticed, and she wore tennis shoes. She wasn't dressed showy, like many of the college kids trying to get attention, and quite often trying to get *his* attention. In fact, she was dressed comfortably and looked more her age, older than the average college student.

Just two years younger than Chad.

"Jess," he said and wasn't surprised when she didn't turn around. His voice came out barely above a whisper because his heart was lodged in his throat.

But he wasn't giving up that easily.

"Jessica," he repeated, maybe a bit too forcefully because she jumped, turned and dropped one of the books from her arms. Arched brows lifted, and those dark, insightful eyes studied him. Obviously startled, her mouth gaped for a moment before she recovered. And smiled.

He had really missed that smile.

"Chad."

Occasionally, at unique instances in his life, Chad's medical studies came back to haunt him. Right now ended up being one of those moments. Because he suddenly recalled the result of a surge of epinephrine, or adrenaline. *When produced in the body, it increases heart rate, contracts blood vessels and dilates air passages.* All of that was happening right now, and even with his med school knowledge, he wasn't sure how to handle it.

"What…what are you doing here?" she asked, scooping up the lost book and tucking it back against her chest.

Her question jolted him back to reality. What was *he* doing here? He wasn't the one who'd left town so long ago—six years ago.

A lifetime ago.

"I teach here," he said and was thankful that his voice remained calm. What he wanted to do was grab her and shake her, ask her why she'd come back—and more importantly, why she'd waited so long. "Now, your turn."

"We…I…" Color tinged her cheeks, and she cleared her throat. "I'm sorry. I didn't expect to see you. You're teaching? Here? I thought you were living in Georgia, going to school at the University of Georgia. Or wait, Emory?" Her words came out in a rush, a slight quiver with occasional syllables, as though she were cold. Well, of course she was cold; it was January. But Chad didn't think that was what made her voice shake. Jessica's voice always trembled when she was nervous. She was nervous now. He wondered if she was feeling even an iota of the apprehension that he felt, being this close to her after they'd been apart for so long. "The bachelor's degree at UGA and med school at Emory, right?" she completed.

So she'd kept up with him. He'd attempted to keep

up with her way back when, but she wouldn't return his calls or even tell him exactly where she went. He'd learned from his sister that she moved to Tennessee to live with her grandmother, but he didn't know where in Tennessee, and he sure didn't know why. Basically, Jessica Bowman, the girl he'd planned to marry, had left Claremont, Alabama—and him—without a backward glance.

"I was at Emory, but I came back home last year. Well, close to home. I bought a house on the Stockville side of Claremont. I'm still near Mom, so I can help her if she needs me, and I have an easy drive to work." He was rambling. It had been six years since he'd seen her, and here he was talking about the drive to work. He wanted to smack himself in the head and tell himself to get a grip. But he didn't. Instead, he stood there, with Jessica again, and attempted to act as though it were completely normal to run into his first love on the Stockville campus.

"One of the new subdivisions?" she asked. "I noticed them when I came in. They're very nice. It's something, isn't it? When I left, there were only cotton fields on the edge of town. Now there are entire neighborhoods. I guess a lot of things can change in six years."

A major understatement. A lot of things *had* changed, but one thing hadn't. He wasn't the type of guy to skirt an issue back then, and he wasn't going to start now. He wanted answers to lots of questions, but he'd start with the basics.

"Jess, when did you come back? Where are you living? When did you leave Tennessee? And why are you here, on campus?"

She blinked, moistened her mouth and then ran her

top teeth across her lower lip, like she always did when she was avoiding something.

What didn't she want to tell him?

"I moved back last week, and I'm staying with my parents until I find a place of my own. They paid my tuition to the college as a Christmas present. They wanted me to go back to school. I started my classes today."

Two women hurried across the quad toward them, and Chad and Jess moved to one side to let them pass.

"Hello, Mr. Martin," one of the girls said.

"Ladies," he acknowledged, recognizing the speaker as a girl who had taken his summer course last year.

The other girl waved at Jess. "Hey, it was nice to meet you. See you next week."

"Okay," Jess said, then looked at Chad. "She was in my last class. It seems kind of strange to be back in school again but in a good way. Luckily, they were only a few days into the semester when I registered. My instructors said I should be able to catch up without any problems." She visibly swallowed, her slender throat pulsing with the motion.

Chad wanted to slide his hand beneath the edge of that fuzzy scarf and feel that pulse for himself, to prove that she was really here and that he wasn't merely dreaming again.

"I'm still hoping to be a teacher eventually, but right now I'm working in a day care center. Actually, I got the job today. I start on Tuesday," she added, another warm puff of air escaping her mouth with the words.

Chad watched that wispy air fade away, as quickly as she'd faded from his life years ago. It was a reminder of how she'd left but also a reminder that this time she was real. And she was here with him.

"I can see you teaching." He had envisioned that very thing, her teaching kindergarten and the kids looking at her and thinking she was the best part of their day. He'd felt the same way about his kindergarten teacher; he'd bet most kids did. But with Jessica it'd be true.

She was certainly the best part of this day for him.

Shifting her books to one arm, she tucked a thick lock of highlighted honey hair behind her ear and asked, "How about you? I thought you'd be doing, what, an internship or something now in a hospital." She paused, then added softly, "I heard that you married."

Jessica took her gaze from his face to his left hand, wrapped around the handle of his leather briefcase.

The gold band glistened beneath the yellow light.

Chad cleared his throat. He'd forgotten all about the ring. "It's not what you think," he said, indicating the wedding band on his finger.

"It's not?"

He shook his head. "I got divorced last year."

"Oh," she said, her genuine concern evident in the single word. "I'm sorry, Chad." Then confusion etched across her features as she tilted her head toward his hand. "Then, why do you wear the ring?"

"Like I said, it isn't what you think," he said and shrugged as he smiled. "I'm a good deal younger than the average college professor, not much older than my students, and the ring helps keep the freshman girls in line."

Her amused look embarrassed him a bit, and he added, "One of the other instructors suggested it, and it does work."

"Well, at least they have the decency to respect a marriage vow, even if it is a farce."

A farce. That'd be a good way to describe his marriage to Kate. But he wouldn't think about that now, now that Jessica had come home. To Claremont? Or to him?

Well, of course to Claremont. She'd clearly been surprised to see him here tonight, and she'd thought he was still married. She hadn't returned to him back then and she hadn't now.

Even so, she was here now, and Chad wasn't about to waste the opportunity to find out what had happened to her since she'd left. Naturally, there was one thing he wanted to know, *had* to know, before his heart started hoping again. And—like he told his students—you can't get an answer if you don't ask the question.

"How about you?" he heard himself ask. "Have you married?"

Chad's prayer life hadn't been what it used to be before the divorce, but he said a silent one now.

Please, God, let her say no.

Jessica had heard people discuss experiences where it seemed as though they were merely watching life occur around them, where an individual wasn't actually participating in the event but an onlooker, observing the activity and wondering how the scene would play out. She'd never experienced anything like that herself—until now.

Chad Martin. Of all the people she thought she might run into on this small college campus, his name wouldn't have even been on the list. But if she could list the one person she'd want to see more than any other, his name would undoubtedly be the one. She'd thought he would still be in med school. She'd thought he would still be married.

Divorced? Chad? Why would anyone blessed enough to have Chad Martin for a husband ever let him go?

It'd been six long years since she'd seen him, and she hoped the darkness surrounding them hid the way she couldn't stop studying every feature of the boy—now a man—that she'd first loved. He'd worn his hair in a crisp, short cut in high school. Now it was a bit longer, and she noticed that there was more of a wave to the streaks of sandy brown than she remembered. He seemed taller, too, at least six-one or maybe even six-two. Had he been that tall back then?

His jawline was exactly as she remembered, firm and straight, a little angled, so that he almost appeared to be clenching. But in a good way. A very nice, very good way.

She swallowed, then looked at the feature she remembered better than any other. Deep, forest-green eyes that seemed to pierce through to her very soul, and the tiny gold flecks within that sea of green that caught the illumination of the light surrounding them and made him look as though he'd harnessed a bit of fire and held it captive inside his soul.

"Jess? I asked if you'd married," he repeated, those intriguing eyes examining her carefully as he spoke.

She snapped back to the conversation. Married. The only man she'd ever wanted to marry was standing in front of her.

"No, I didn't."

His head tilted slightly, not really a nod but more of a questioning motion. And then Chad being Chad asked, "Why not?"

She couldn't help it; she laughed. "You still say whatever you want, whenever you want, don't you? You always said if you wanted to know something you simply asked, and people told you."

He grinned, and the deep dimple in his left cheek winked at her. "Hey, it usually works." Then he raised a dark brow. "So, why not?"

"I guess because the right person never asked." She swallowed and wondered if she'd given too much away with that remark. The right one would have asked, she knew, if she'd told him the truth six years ago.

He took a small step forward, closer. "Jess, a lot happened back then, but I never really knew why you felt like you had to leave. Why wouldn't you return my calls? Or tell me exactly where you were?"

"You were going off to school," she said simply. "And I needed to get away."

"Without saying goodbye? To me?" He shook his head. "It never made sense then, and it doesn't now. Tell me the truth, Jess."

Her heart thudded so hard she was certain she could feel it against her ribs. The truth. The truth was beautiful, wonderful, alive and exciting…and there was no way she could blurt it out now.

How would he ever forgive her?

"I told you, Chad, I needed to get away." She glanced toward the parking lot. "And I really should go now. It's late—" she shivered "—and cold."

"I'm sorry. I shouldn't have kept you out here this long," he said, as caring and thoughtful as he'd always been. "But I'm glad you're back, and I'm glad I saw you tonight."

"Me, too." She turned to go but knew that she wouldn't

be able to walk away that easily. Chad wanted to know more about why she left six years ago, and he wasn't the type of guy to give up when he wanted to know something.

"Jess?"

She took a deep breath of cool air, then turned back toward those green and gold eyes. "Yes?"

"It's been a long time, but I still have a lot of questions about what happened, and I want to talk."

She owed him that. Then she winced, recalling how he'd called her repeatedly and left her message after message telling her how much he cared for her, how much he loved her. She owed him more than a talk. She owed him the truth. "Okay."

"What time do your classes end tomorrow?" he asked.

"Tomorrow's Friday. Stockville doesn't have classes on Friday, professor." She winked at him, and he shook his head, obviously embarrassed by his mistake. Clearly, this meeting was as awkward for him as it was for her.

"I'll tell you the truth, Jess. Seeing you tonight has kind of thrown my world off kilter. I'd thought, well, I guess I thought I'd never see you again."

Jessica knew exactly what he meant. But he would have seen her, whenever she got the courage to find him and tell him…everything.

"So let me try again," he continued. "I'm assuming you just got out of class at seven-thirty, so is that the end of your day for Tuesdays and Thursdays?"

She nodded. "I'm taking one Monday-Wednesday class, so I'm done at five on those days. Taking two Tuesday-Thursday classes, so I finish up at seven-thirty."

"Tuesdays and Thursdays are my late nights, too," he said. "There's a little coffee and danish shop down the street. Would you want to go there after you finish your classes on Tuesday?"

She hesitated, ran her teeth across her lower lip. If she went home right after her last class, she might get a chance to put Nathan to bed. He was still getting used to his new bed, so she really didn't want to leave him to go to sleep without a good night kiss. "What about Tuesday afternoon, before my class?"

"I have classes straight through from noon until seven-thirty."

"Oh." She needed to talk to him, and she was certain that there was a reason she'd run into him on this campus. She was a big believer in God's plan, and she knew that He wouldn't have placed her here with Chad again unless she was supposed to do something. Who was she kidding? She knew what she needed to do. What she didn't know was…how.

"I promise I won't keep you long. A half hour," he said.

"A half hour would be okay, I suppose." She smiled, and turned to go again, already pondering how she would tell him the truth.

But Chad's next words caused her to stop completely.

"I have a daughter."

Jessica's breath caught in her throat, and she had to replay the words to process them completely.

"I have a daughter." A *daughter.*

Gaining her composure, she turned back toward him.

"Her name is Lainey, and she's, well, pretty amazing."

He smiled, the obvious pride he felt for his child undeniable in the statement.

Jessica's eyes started to tingle, and she prayed he'd believe the tears were from the cold. "I'm very happy for you," she said. "I'm sure she's extremely amazing." Then she swallowed, cleared her throat and said exactly what she hadn't planned to say to him tonight. "I have a son."

The shock on his face matched hers upon learning that he had a little girl.

"You have a son?"

Jess nodded and smiled, her cheeks pressing upward and causing that tiny river of tears to spill over. Again, she prayed he thought it was from the cold. "His name is Nathan." Then she laughed and added, "And he's pretty amazing, too."

"I'm sure he is."

They both stood there for a moment, a bounty of words and explanations tumbling through her thoughts but none spoken.

Then, after several heartbeats of standing there in that cool January air, Chad broke the uncomfortable silence.

"So coffee, Tuesday after class? And we'll catch up on everything we've missed."

"Yes, we will," she said, her words barely above a whisper as a result of the lump in her throat. Then she moved away from Chad Martin, away from the only man she'd ever loved and away from the man whose eyes were identical to the ones she'd see when she returned home…to his son.

Chapter Two

Jessica drove mechanically back to Claremont, her mind processing the magnitude of what she'd learned on campus tonight. Chad was an instructor at Stockville Community College. He'd moved back to Claremont and was teaching. She shook her head at that. He'd wanted that medical degree so much. Why had he given up on that dream?

She'd kept her pregnancy from him to protect that dream, to make certain that he achieved that goal first before she told him about their son. Then when she'd come back to Claremont three years ago to tell him about Nathan, Chad's sister Becky had said he was done at UGA, that he'd actually gotten his bachelor's degree in three years and that he was going to Emory for med school and getting married. That was the last time Jess had spoken to her old friend, since Becky had also married and moved away with her army husband. She'd heard they were stationed in Alaska. And when Becky moved so far away, the two friends had lost touch without Jessica ever telling her friend she was an aunt… or telling Chad he was a daddy.

And Jess had consequently lost her primary link to Nathan's father.

Some time after that trip home, Chad returned to Claremont, had a daughter and got a divorce.

A divorce. Chad had confided in her repeatedly through their teen years about how much it hurt growing up without two parents and how he'd marry for life, that he'd do whatever it took to make his marriage work and that if he had children, he'd never, ever want them to go through life without parents who cared about them and without love in the home.

Yet he'd divorced. What had happened? What would have caused him to separate from his wife? Had she left him? Was she still living in Claremont? Becky had told her that Chad met his wife in Atlanta, while he was attending Emory. Maybe she was used to big cities and couldn't handle small-town life? No, Jess thought. They wouldn't have moved back to Claremont if that had been the case.

So many questions and not a single answer to be found. Yet he wanted them to get together for coffee so they could chat about what happened when she left six years ago. Well, Jessica wanted to chat, too, and learn what happened in the six years since—specifically, what happened to the marriage that had kept her from telling Chad about Nathan three years ago.

Again, Jess shook her head in disbelief. Why would anyone leave Chad? Maybe his wife had hurt him, so much that he simply couldn't stay with her. And Chad apparently had custody of their daughter.

A daughter. Chad had a daughter and, according to him, she was "pretty amazing."

Tears trickled down her cheeks. The delight he'd

expressed when telling Jess about the little girl pierced her heart. It wasn't that she was upset he had a child with someone else. The thing was, he didn't realize that he had a pretty amazing son, too. He didn't know because Jessica still hadn't told him.

She wondered if the little girl, Lainey, looked like Nathan. Did she act like him? Did Chad get to watch her blond baby fuzz hair turn sandy and wavy, so much like his own? Or the blue eyes she'd been born with change to that stunning deep forest-green, with the tiny gold flecks and ring of dark brown around the edge. Were her eyes inquisitive, like Nathan's, always searching for answers, examining every tiny nuance of life around them?

Jessica suddenly had an immeasurable longing to see his daughter, get to know her and introduce her to Nathan. She wondered how old Lainey was, and she was instantly touched by the fact that Nathan was a big brother. He'd often asked her for a little brother or sister who he could teach things to. At the time, she'd tried to let him down easy, since that was nowhere near a possibility when she'd had no interest in dating; she'd only wanted to raise her son, for the time being. She'd thought maybe, someday, she'd find love again, but it certainly had been a distant dream. And in her heart, she wasn't sure she could ever truly love anyone but Chad.

She passed the sign that said Welcome to Claremont at the edge of town and followed the familiar roads leading home. She noticed the new subdivisions, houses on cul-de-sacs where cotton fields had once been. Square beams of light shone from the windows of the homes on the winding streets.

Chad lived in one of those houses. Chad—and his daughter.

At some point between Stockville and Claremont, it had started to rain. With the darkness and the water streaming in wet sheets down her windshield, she was taken back to the last time she'd seen Chad Martin. She'd driven to his house to tell him that they were going to have a baby, and she knew it'd be tough, but she'd known that the two of them would find a way to make it work. They'd get married and start their family.

But he'd had big news that night, too. And after he told her that he'd gotten the scholarship he'd dreamed of, a full ride to the University of Georgia, she simply couldn't tell him about the baby. And she'd driven home in the rain, crying the whole way. Then she'd called him and told him a lie.

The rain fell harder, and she slowly pulled her car into the driveway, then darted to the house. And like that night six years ago, her mother was waiting in the living room, sitting on the couch and staring at the door expectantly. The last time she'd been waiting to see whether Jessica would agree to move to Tennessee, live with her grandmother and have her baby. This time she was waiting for something else, and Jess didn't think it was merely to see how her classes went in Stockville.

"So, how was your night?" Anna Bowman asked, leaning forward on the couch. "How were your classes? Did you see anyone you know?" Her cheeks flushed slightly, and she clarified, "I thought, you know, with the campus being so close to Claremont and all, that you might have run into some of your old classmates."

Jess suddenly realized that there was more going on here than she'd originally thought, more to her parents' interest in sending her to the college.

They knew.

"Where's Nathan?" she asked, trying to tamp down on her shock and control her voice.

"Your father is reading him a story before bed," her mother said and smiled, but it didn't quite meet her eyes.

Jessica crossed the room, sat in the oak rocking chair that had been her grandmother's and began to slowly rock back and forth while she let her mind play over everything that had happened in the past few weeks. Her parents had called her in Tennessee and told her how much they wanted her to bring Nathan back here for school. She'd thought about it for a few days, a little hesitant about moving in the middle of the school year, but finally deciding that she wanted to do that, too, raise him in her hometown and near his grandparents. She wanted him to have some sense of a real family. But then they'd also wanted her to go back to school, and they'd wanted her to go to the community college in Stockville rather than the one in Claremont. They even paid her first semester's tuition as a Christmas present.

"How long have you known?" she asked softly.

A slight flush whispered up her mother's throat. "Known what?"

"That Chad was divorced and moved back here and that he was teaching at Stockville."

Her mother cleared her throat. "Oh, well, you know how small towns are." She waved her hands slightly as she spoke. "Everybody talks when someone comes back to town. Your father and I thought you might want an opportunity to see him again, maybe talk to him and tell him about Nathan."

She'd always planned to tell Chad about their son. That's why she'd returned three years ago, but then she'd learned he was about to get married and she'd returned to her grandmother's farm in Tennessee. But she'd always intended to tell him, and she assumed God would let her know when the time was right.

Evidently, He thought the time was right now, and He let her parents help set things in motion.

"So, you saw Chad tonight?" her mother asked.

"Yes."

"We were planning to help you go back to school one day anyway," she explained. "But when we heard he was teaching at Stockville we thought that was a sign we should send you there. God works in mysterious ways," her mother added, smiling. "You forgive us for not telling you the whole story?"

"I do," Jessica said. How could she be upset with them for wanting their grandson to know his father? But she wondered if Chad would ever forgive her for not telling him about his son. Soon, she suspected, she'd know, whenever she gained enough courage to tell him the truth. For now, though, she'd go see the other guy with green-gold eyes who held a large piece of her heart.

She hugged her mom, told her that she was sure everything would work out the way it was supposed to and then headed upstairs.

The door to the guest room, Nathan's room for now, was cracked open. She approached quietly and peered inside, eager to see the interaction between Nathan and his granddaddy. Nathan hadn't had a father figure in his world so far, and he hadn't spent nearly as much time with her father as she would've liked, so this scene was very special.

Her son sat against the headboard, his sandy curls leaning against her father's side as Nathan pointed to a page of the book his granddaddy held. He tilted his head up and raised his brows, the same face he always gave Jessica when he expected her to answer one of his intricate questions.

Nathan never accepted anything at face value. Even at two, he was determined to learn exactly how his toy train whistled and took the thing completely apart, to the point that Jessica couldn't even attempt to put it back together. He wanted to know how things worked, why things happened, what caused what in the entire scheme of things. He was inquisitive, intelligent and witty. Never afraid to ask what he wanted to know. In other words, he was his father's son, and Jessica couldn't have been more pleased.

She recalled Chad's blunt query from earlier tonight.

"Have you married?" And then *"Why not?"*

Tough questions, for sure, but she was used to tough questions. She got them often enough from Nathan. And he wasn't cutting her father any slack now.

She stepped into the room in time to hear him ask, "But *how* did the stone knock his head off?"

Her father's smile, and his adoration for his grandson, was absolutely breathtaking. And he didn't get frustrated by Nathan's confusion. Instead, he appeared to enjoy that Nathan wanted facts about the story. "You see, God was helping David, and that's how the stone knocked off the giant's head. Or rather, the stone knocked him down and then David cut off his head with a sword."

Nathan's small hands instinctively moved to grasp his head.

"No one would want to hurt your head, so you have nothing to worry about," her dad said with a low chuckle

Nathan squinted at his granddaddy, then apparently noticed Jessica's presence and shifted gears in the subject matter to what he knew was the most important item in her day. "Hey, Mama. Did you get it? Get that job you wanted?"

She'd called home and told her parents about the position at the day care center right after the interview. Apparently, they hadn't thought her little guy would be interested in her news, which proved they still had a lot to learn about their grandson. Nathan was interested in *everything,* and she loved that about him, just like she loved it about his Daddy.

"Well, did you?" Nathan repeated.

"I did," she said, opening her arms and waiting, while he jumped off the bed and ran to give her his traditional welcome home hug. She inhaled his little boy smell—chocolate chip cookies with a hint of soap from his bath—and squeezed him tightly.

"Hey, I can't breathe!"

Laughing, she released her hold and placed him on the bed, where he crawled back to his spot beneath the covers.

"Sorry. I missed you," she said.

"Missed you, too," he said, "But maybe you won't miss me too much while I'm at big school if you have all those little kids to take care of," he said, happily putting himself in the "big kid" category.

"Yeah, those little ones need someone to take care of them, for sure," she agreed, enjoying the way his eyes beamed at her, and the way the gold flecks sparkled within the deep sea of green. She'd never gotten tired of those eyes six years ago, when she'd fallen in love with Chad Martin. And she sure didn't get tired of them now.

"Now that you're going to work, Granddaddy says I can take the bus and it will pick me up right outside, by the mailbox." Nathan pointed out the window toward the end of the driveway, where that big gold bus always picked up Jessica when she was his age. "And he said he'll wait with me in the morning and that MeMaw will help me pack my new Superman lunch box for school." Exactly what they'd done with Jessica, except her lunch box had had Malibu Barbie on the front.

"What new Superman lunch box?"

"The one MeMaw bought him at Walmart today, I suppose," her father said, grinning.

"I got new Superman shoes, too," Nathan announced. "For school."

"Sounds like MeMaw is spoiling you rotten." Jessica cocked her head at her dad.

"Don't look at me," he said. "You know I'd have said no."

"Sure you would've," Jess said, spying an empty glass with a hint of milk at the bottom and a crumb-covered plate on the nightstand, which explained why Nathan had smelled like chocolate chip cookies.

"You're getting me the backpack, Granddaddy," Nathan said. "Remember?"

Her father shrugged. "Okay, guilty."

"Let's stop the madness at the backpack," Jessica said, pressing a finger against Nathan's nose.

"They've got Superman notebooks, too," Nathan mumbled. Then he looked at his granddaddy and grinned. "And pencils."

"Well, you certainly can't have the backpack and not

get the matching notebooks and pencils, can you?" her father asked.

"You might as well hang it up, Jess," her mother said, stepping into the room. "We're hopeless and are bound and determined to spoil him rotten." She smiled. "But that's our job."

"Yep, that's their job," Nathan agreed, smiling broadly and showcasing the empty hole where a tiny baby tooth used to be.

Jessica's heart tensed. He was growing up way too fast.

"And I'll catch the bus right out there," he said, informing MeMaw of the bit of conversation she'd missed earlier. "Until we get our new house. And then I'll ride it from there."

Jessica had moved in with her folks until she could find a place of her own, and she had been up front with Nathan about that plan. She didn't want him getting too attached to living with his grandparents, and she hadn't wanted them to get too attached to having her and Nathan here either. She was twenty-three and didn't want to mooch off of her parents forever.

However, she had to admit that being with them now and seeing them enjoy having her and Nathan here was very nice.

"I see," her mother said, sitting on the bed beside her husband. They looked so good together, so content after all of these years, sitting there with Nathan, and Jessica suddenly had a sense of exactly what was missing in her life.

Then Nathan giggled, and she remembered that her life was fine. No, not what she'd planned, but A-OK for now. And she'd seen Nathan's daddy tonight and also learned that Nathan had a little sister. On Tuesday, she'd talk to Chad, maybe even tell him about their little boy.

Excitement bubbled within her. Excitement…and fear.

God, help me be strong enough to tell him. And God, please, let him understand.

Chad Martin woke up bright and early Friday morning. Or to be more precise, he gave up on any hope of a decent night's sleep at around 5:00 a.m. He'd dozed off and on, but whether his eyes were open or closed, his mind wouldn't stop running through the events of last night, from the moment he saw the woman walking across the quad to the moment he realized that Jessica was really back in Claremont.

Really back in his life.

She was as pretty as she was back then—prettier—with silky chocolate hair, dark brown eyes and that cute little nose that wrinkled when she laughed. And when she laughed, her mouth was soft and subtle, easily finding its way into a smile. Jess had a smile that took his breath away. There was something so genuine about it, as though the whole world should look a little brighter when she grinned. It simply made him feel good inside to see that smile.

But it wasn't merely her physical appearance that attracted Chad to Jess so much, though she was the most naturally attractive female he'd ever met. There was a fresh, honest appeal to Jessica Bowman. She was the kind of girl who could not only be your best friend, the one you could open your soul to, but also the kind of girl you could love—for life. He'd sensed that in her when they were teens, from the time she started coming over to their house, first as Becky's friend. And then, as she grew older, and as she and Chad talked and grew closer, as Chad's first true love.

He followed the strong scent of coffee to the kitchen and was thankful he'd taken the time to set the automatic brew feature the night before. Pretty incredible that he remembered, given how shaken he'd been from Jessica's reappearance into his world. He'd even forgotten the day of the week when he'd asked what time she finished class today. That was one of the things he loved about the community college, the fact that every week was a four-day deal, giving him Fridays to truly enjoy his daughter.

And speaking of his little girl, Lainey would wake up soon, and Chad needed to be ready. She was eighteen months old now, toddling around and talking baby speak and quite a handful.

Chad loved every minute of it.

Grabbing a University of Georgia mug, he filled the cup with coffee, moved to his back window and enjoyed the strong taste against his palette. He thought about Lainey and how much he enjoyed his little girl. And then he remembered Jessica's words.

"I have a son."

Jessica had a little boy. Chad had been so stunned at the news that he hadn't asked any of the normal questions. Now he wondered how old he was. What was he like? Did he look like Jess? And naturally he wondered who was the little guy's father? And why hadn't Jess married him? He couldn't fathom her having a baby out of marriage, not after the conversations they had back in high school about that very thing. Particularly that one conversation on the night she left town.

The baby monitor on the kitchen counter crackled as Lainey sighed in her sleep. She was probably getting ready to start stirring, and she'd want her juice as soon as she opened her eyes. Chad took another sip of his coffee, then set the mug on the counter, grabbed her pink Minnie Mouse sippy cup and filled it with apple juice. Next he scanned the kitchen until he spotted her pacifier on the table. He took it to the sink, rinsed it off and then placed it next to the sippy cup.

Fridays were fun days for Chad, days to really take the time to see what Lainey had learned throughout the week, hear whatever new words she was saying and watch her toddle around and explore the world. He was anxious for the weather to get warm enough to take her to Hydrangea Park and feed the ducks. It wouldn't be long, thanks to Alabama's mild winters, and he couldn't wait.

Another soft mumble echoed through the baby monitor, and Chad knew his little girl was starting to rouse. He took another sip of coffee and watched the first rays of sunlight break through the night. The sky immediately took on an array of colors with the brilliant addition. Purples and pinks, oranges and golds.

Chad sipped more coffee and thought how quickly the sun's rays had changed the sky's disposition, shifting it in one broad stroke from dismal gray and black to a kaleidoscope of vivid hues. He'd say the new morning sky looked rather heavenly, like a painting from God.

A frown tugged at his mouth, and he sighed. God had painted his life a bit differently than the one he'd envisioned, the one that included a happy home and a medical degree. But he was a firm believer that things happen for a reason, for God's reason, and even though he hadn't been on the best of terms with Him for the past few years, Chad was trying to get back on the right track again, slowly but surely. He and Lainey had even made it to a couple of church services, and it didn't feel so awkward, as though everyone was staring at them and feeling pity toward him and his life.

True, it wasn't what he'd planned, but he'd work it out the best way he knew how. And right now, the best way he knew how involved teaching biology at the community college and being with Lainey.

The sun had moved up to a half globe now, a red-orange mass that pressed outward and pushed the black away, changing everything in its path from dark and gloomy to bright and cheery.

This was part of Chad's morning ritual, watching the sun rise from his kitchen window, and he was certain it had probably looked this incredible several other days as well. But today, he saw the image more clearly, and he saw it as a symbol, perhaps a sign from God, that his dark, gloomy life was changing. A ray of sunlight found its way through the darkness last night, when Jessica walked back into his life again, and Chad found, like the sky that he currently watched out his window, that everything around him looked brighter.

A tiny little grunt, followed by the sound of rustling sheets, emitted through the baby monitor told him that Lainey was waking up. He set his coffee mug on the counter and picked up the sippy cup and pacifier. Then he started down the hall.

"Dada," she said, her tiny voice whimpering.

He grinned. Only eighteen months old and already

she knew she wasn't a morning person. She was like her mother that way. Kate didn't "do" mornings. With Kate, it'd been a bit irritating.

With Lainey, it was cute.

He rounded the corner and walked into her room, where his little lady stood inside of her crib, her small fists clenched tightly around the railing, her big blue eyes staring unblinking at the door and awaiting his arrival, and her blond curls, as always, standing on end, wild and crazy with her adorable bedhead. Dora the Explorer covered the new pink fleece pajamas he'd bought her earlier this week. He'd thought the way the feet were built into the pajamas would keep her toes warm, since she often worked her way out of her tiny socks at night. But right now, she held up one foot as though the feature was more of a nuisance than a benefit.

"Good morning, sunshine," he said, holding up the juice and pacifier so she could see he'd brought what she wanted and consequently, she wouldn't feel the need to start crying for them. And maybe that'd make her forget about her problem with his choice for her nightwear.

"Duuuce," she said, and reached for the sippy cup.

Chad obligingly handed it over.

She took a big sip, noisily slurping her little pink lips around the tiny holes in the top of the cup. Then she swallowed, moved the cup away from her mouth and held out her other hand. "Pappy."

Chad put the pacifier in her hand. She balled her fist around it and gave him her trademark baby-tooth grin. "Tank oo."

"You're welcome," he said, scooping her up and nuzzling the blond fuzzy curls away so he could kiss her cheek and neck.

Lainey ducked her chin to her neck trying to fend off her Daddy's kisses and giggled. "Wuv you."

"I love you, too," Chad said. And he did love everything about her—her blond curls, her baby blue eyes, her adorable mouth. He realized, as he often did, that everything about her resembled Kate. There wasn't a trace of Chad's features in this little angel. But resembling Kate physically was as far as it went. Because Lainey's brilliant blue eyes were sweet and innocent, not manipulative and cold. Lainey's smile was real, not fake.

And when Lainey told him she loved him, she meant it.

Chapter Three

Jessica wondered if everyone experienced the same mesmerized sensation when they returned to the church of their youth. She'd grown up sitting in the pews within the steepled white building at least three times each week, and then after seventeen years of knowing nothing but this church, she left. Returning, she was welcomed by an abundance of wide smiles and welcoming arms, with everyone admiring her little boy and telling her how nice it was that she'd come back home. And that was before she stepped one foot in the door.

Walking across the parking lot, she was bombarded by old friends. She imagined that this was something similar to what the prodigal son felt when he saw his father running toward him down the road, except it was Brother Henry, her preacher, who ran toward her now. Well, okay, he wasn't running, but he moved faster than she'd ever seen Brother Henry move before.

The preacher's hair had grayed completely in the years since she'd left Claremont, and his face appeared more weathered, with the smile lines bordering his mouth more pronounced than she remembered and additional crinkle marks at the corners of his eyes. His brows were stark white, drawing attention to the pale blue of those kind eyes.

"Jessica! It's so good to have you back. And this must be Nathan," he said, leaning down to ruffle Nathan's sandy waves.

"Yes, sir," Nathan said, giving him a crooked, squinting-in-the-sunlight smile.

"Your grandparents have told me all about you," Brother Henry said. "They're very proud of you."

"Yep, they are," Nathan agreed, which caused a laugh from both Brother Henry and Jessica's parents, following them up the steps.

"So, Nathan," Brother Henry continued, "has anyone ever told you what your name means in Hebrew? From the Bible? Because there was a Nathan in the Bible, too."

"Mom told me Nathan was in the Bible," he said, and Jessica felt a surge of pride that she'd made an impression. "He told King David what was going to happen." Nathan tilted his head toward his grandfather and said, "That must've been after David cut off that giant's head, huh?"

"Definitely," her father said, beaming and apparently quite proud that his grandson was so quickly putting his Bible facts together.

"Very good," Brother Henry said. "Nathan was a prophet, and he did tell King David the things that would happen in the future. Your mommy taught you well. And did she tell you what the name means?"

"No, she didn't," Jessica said with a grin, "because she didn't know." She'd merely selected the name because it was the only one in the books of baby names that seemed to be *right* for her son. Now she wondered exactly why it seemed so right.

"Well, it means 'God has given,'" Brother Henry said.

Jessica's throat tightened. God *had* given Nathan to her, and even his name was proof of the fact.

"Neat!" Nathan said, then repeated, "God has given. That's my name."

"That's right," Brother Henry agreed, still smiling at him. He pulled a peppermint out of his suit pocket and handed it to Nathan. "This is to keep your tummy from growling in church," he said, then winked. "I'd have one, too, but it's hard for me to preach with candy in my mouth."

Nathan laughed at that. "Can I have another one for class?"

"Nathan." Jessica gave Brother Henry an embarrassed shrug.

But Brother Henry tousled his hair again and said, "Tell you what. After church, I'm going to ask you what I talked about. If you can tell me, I'll give you another one." He nodded toward Jessica's parents. "Maybe I'll have at least one person listening to the sermon that way."

"Give me a peppermint, and I'll listen, too," Jessica's father said, which made them all laugh.

They entered the foyer, and Jessica felt the first inkling of curiosity from the other side of the lobby. A couple of the older women were huddled, hands over their mouths and whispering as they glanced at Jessica—and more pointedly at Nathan.

Jessica protectively put her arm around his little shoulders and steered him toward the classroom hall. She'd known she wouldn't get prodigal son treatment from everyone, but that was okay; even the prodigal son's brother had a hard time with his return.

Class was pretty much status quo for what she remembered, but Brother Henry's church service was much different than the type she recalled from growing up. A lot less fire and brimstone, a lot more grace. Jessica commented on the change to her parents as they walked out of the auditorium.

Her father agreed. "I was wondering if you'd notice. Brother Henry did a summer series on grace a couple of years back, said the more he studied on the subject, the more he thought we'd gone way too long leaving it out of the equation."

Jess turned to see what her mother thought of the change, but she was completely ignoring their conversation and scanning the congregation, pleasantly visiting in small huddles as they slowly moved toward the back of the building. "Mom, you looking for someone?"

"Yes," she said, then shook her head. "No, not really. I'd noticed last week that we had some other folks visiting again who'd been away for a while, and I'd hoped they'd be back today."

"Who?" Jessica asked. Like most people in Claremont, she knew almost everyone in town—or at least knew who their family was.

"Oh, look," her father said. "Nathan's going for the peppermint."

They all turned and walked toward Brother Henry, standing at the doorway shaking hands with everyone and preparing to shake Nathan's outstretched hand. But Nathan's palm was turned up, waiting for another piece of candy.

"Please?" he said, his *s* lisping a little due to his missing tooth.

"Hey, we had a deal, remember?" Brother Henry lifted a white brow.

"I remember," Nathan said. "And I listened to you preaching."

"Okay, what did I talk about?" He crouched down to Nathan's level.

Jessica was curious as to whether Nathan had actually heard. He'd spent the majority of the service admiring his Superman shoes, which he'd told Jessica were "nice enough to wear with church clothes because they're brand-new." She'd let him win that one, deciding to choose her battles, even though the colorful tennis shoes didn't exactly go with his khaki pants and striped navy sweater.

"You talked about daddies," Nathan said matter-of-factly.

Jessica's world seemed to stall for a moment. "Daddies?" she asked, her voice a little raspy at hearing Nathan say the word so sweetly.

Nathan's head bobbed. "Yep, how much daddies love their children and how God loves us the same way. That's what you said."

Jessica wasn't certain, but she thought Brother Henry's chin wobbled a bit before he worked his mouth back into a smile. "That's exactly right," he said, then visibly swallowed and handed Nathan the striped candy.

Brother Henry stood from where he'd knelt down to speak to Nathan, and this time she was sure that she saw a bit of moisture in his eyes, which matched the dampness in her own.

"It's good to have both of you here, Jessica," he said, the warmness in his tone touching her heart.

"It's good to be back."

She, Nathan and her parents walked quietly toward her father's car, then all piled inside and buckled up for the ride back home for her mother's traditional Sunday pot roast. But food wasn't on Jessica's mind, and she suspected it wasn't on her parents' minds either.

On the contrary, Nathan's words to Brother Henry were resonating through her thoughts, and her son wasn't done discussing the lesson.

"Mommy?"

"Yes."

"Did you hear him talk about daddies?"

She breathed in deeply, let it out slowly. "I sure did."

Nathan nodded, and Jessica sighed with relief. Maybe that was it.

And maybe cows would fly. This was Nathan, and he wasn't done figuring everything out yet.

"Mommy?"

She noticed her mother shift uncomfortably in the front seat, place a hand over her mouth and peer out the passenger window and she assumed this conversation was going to be as rough for her parents as it was for her. Or close. "Yes?"

He continued looking out his window as he spoke so Jessica couldn't see his face. And thank goodness, he couldn't see hers, because it was very tough to control her pain at his next words.

"Do all daddies love their kids?"

Have mercy, what would she do now? Did all daddies? If she told him yes, she'd be lying, she knew. Some didn't.

Some weren't good, and that hurt her very soul, but she knew one who would love his son very much, if he knew the truth.

"Your daddy will love you," she said, and she saw both of her parents straighten in their seats. But she couldn't let him believe, not for one minute, that his father wouldn't love him, wouldn't want him, if he knew about him. She'd told him before that his daddy lived somewhere else and that he'd see him one day. That'd been enough to satisfy his mind, before he was nearly six, and before he'd grown up so much.

That wasn't enough anymore.

"It hasn't worked out yet for your daddy to meet you and love you and be a part of your life," she said. "But God has a plan, and one day, He will work it out for you to meet your daddy, and it's going to be a great day." She hoped. And prayed.

Please, God, let it be a great day.

Nathan turned in the seat and his face split into the snaggletoothed grin that she loved and the sweet little dimple in his left cheek reminded her of Chad.

"Will he play baseball with me?"

Jessica blinked through the new moisture around her eyes. "Definitely."

"And take me to eat ice cream?" The gold flecks in those deep green eyes sparkled with excitement.

"Of course."

Nathan nodded again, satisfied, then he twisted back toward the window and whispered, "I'm gonna love him."

Chapter Four

Jessica changed her clothes three times Tuesday afternoon before finally deciding on a green cable sweater, blue jeans and short boots. Not too dressy but nice enough for coffee, she thought. And when Nathan had claimed she looked "very pretty," that was a sign she'd hit the mark. Of course, Nathan always said she looked pretty, even when she'd just woken up, her hair was a mess and she had mascara smears under her eyes. But that was part of his little boy charm, the fact that he believed his mommy was perfect.

She walked across the quad toward her second class and glanced toward the Math and Science building, the building where Chad was most likely teaching his courses. She hadn't thought to ask him what classes he taught, and she'd realized earlier today that she hadn't thought to ask how she would find him after her class. Nor had they exchanged cell numbers in case their plans changed.

She laughed softly. She was way out of practice with the whole guy-girl thing. Then again, the only guy she'd ever had any type of relationship with was Chad. Which was probably why she'd been a bundle of nerves all day.

Thankfully, the fact that it was her first day at the day care center kept her busy enough throughout the morning that she didn't have a lot of time to dwell on the fact that she would be meeting Chad tonight. She'd worked at a church day care center in Tennessee, but it was a much smaller facility than the one in Claremont.

Today she'd assisted in the classroom for four-year-olds, and there had been eighteen kids in the class. Eighteen children, one teacher, one assistant. The ratio of students to teachers was higher than the day care in Tennessee, but she thought that she'd handled the challenge well. In fact, she'd had fun and had ended the day excited about the future when hopefully she'd be the primary teacher in a room full of five-year-old kindergartners like Nathan. Little boys and girls alive with anticipation about learning as much as they could about the world around them, with tons of questions and minds like sponges, eager to soak it all in.

She couldn't wait.

Entering her English Comp class, she took the same seat she'd had last week, in the middle of the front row. Why hide in the back when she really wanted to be up front and center, where it was easier to hear every word without the distractions of other students around her? She was the only one who seemed interested in the front seat anyway, which made her stand out as a bit odd, she supposed.

She also stood out by being early to the class, which didn't seem to be a priority to the majority of the group. At her classes so far, most ambled in at a minute or two until class was supposed to start. And then there were the ones who really didn't care and found their way to class well into the first hour of lecture.

Jessica didn't understand how anyone would be willing to spend the amount of money and time that it took to attend college and then have no enthusiasm whatsoever for the opportunity it provided. But then again, college was probably just the next step to these kids and a choice that had been made by their parents rather than the kids themselves. Jess had always wanted to continue her education and had been disappointed that it didn't appear to be a possibility with the direction her life had taken. So this gift from her folks, the chance to start pursuing her teaching dream, made her truly appreciate the chance to sit right here, in the front row, and learn as much as she could.

"Hey," a girl said, passing by Jessica to sit at a seat halfway back in the next row.

"Hi," Jessica said and realized that it was the same girl who had spoken to her when she was talking to Chad the other night. More students came in, many of them talking about Stockville's basketball team and how they'd fared over the weekend. Jessica hadn't even known the college had a basketball team. And she also was out of the loop on the local band, Fly by Night, who had apparently performed on the quad over the weekend.

It occurred to her that the majority of those around her were eighteen and nineteen, fresh out of high school with nothing to do but hang out and have a good time. At eighteen, she'd had Nathan. At nineteen, she was working a minimum of forty hours at the church day care center and spending every other minute of her time taking care of her baby. If she'd been like all of these kids, she'd have been having a good time and playing.

She smiled to herself knowing she'd had a good time, too. And she'd played, too...with her adorable Nathan. She wouldn't trade one second of it for anything that these other kids were doing.

Her instructor, an older woman with short silver hair, horn-rimmed glasses and a no-nonsense cardigan and pants set, entered the room and dropped a stack of books on the desk with a loud thud. Then she scanned the class, the same way she'd done last week, and nodded. Her attention undeniably landed on Jessica, still the sole front-row student, and a soft smile played with the corners of the woman's wrinkled face.

"Nice to see that someone wants to be here," she mumbled, barely loud enough for Jess to hear, but even so, Jessica was at once glad for her choice of seating.

Then the class proceeded, with Ms. Smelding, the instructor, discussing tonight's topic of writing reflectively, and Jess madly taking notes to make sure she didn't miss anything important.

She was so into the lecture and writing samples that Ms. Smelding provided that she hardly realized two and a half hours had passed when the older woman wrote their next assignment on the dry erase board and dismissed the class.

Gathering her books, Jessica could feel her heart start to race, her skin tingling in anticipation. She hadn't experienced anything like this since high school, but it hadn't been so long that she didn't remember the sensation. Anticipation, that'd be the word to describe the overwhelming emotion of knowing she was going to see the one she loved. Knowing she was going to see Chad.

As if the girls exiting the classroom ahead of her knew exactly what was going through her mind, they acknowledged the object of her nervousness—who was standing outside the room.

"Hello, Mr. Martin," one sang, and several others joined in.

Jess figured that the most popular instructor on campus was the tall, sandy haired one standing outside. No doubt he was more appealing than the ones who'd apparently come out of retirement, like Ms. Smelding.

Back in high school, everyone had eyes for Chad Martin. And that was one of the things that had meant so much to Jessica then, the fact that in spite of the way all of the girls flirted with him, he only had eyes for her and made no secret of his feelings. When she walked out of the classroom tonight and saw him give her that amazing smile, that same old excitement rippled through her.

He's waiting for me.

"Hey," he said, easing away from where he'd been casually leaning against the wall.

"Hi."

His sandy hair was a bit rumpled, and he wore a brown suede blazer over a black crew neck shirt and jeans. It was nice enough to qualify as instructor attire but hip enough to remind Jess that this instructor was extremely young and extremely attractive.

She tried to keep the direction her thoughts had headed from showing on her face. But Chad grinned, and she suspected that just like in high school, he probably knew exactly what she was thinking.

The same group of girls who spoke to him was now walking toward the stairs and turned to look at them.

Jessica knew that look. They wanted to know what was going on between her and the handsome instructor. And they weren't the only ones. She wanted to know what was going on, too, particularly whether Chad could still have some of those old feelings toward her from way back then and then naturally, whether he'd still have them if he knew she'd kept him from his son.

Her palms were damp, throat was tight. She was a nervous wreck.

He stepped toward her. "So how was class? Ms. Smelding tends to be long-winded from what I've heard, and I guess tonight confirms that."

Jess glanced at her watch. The class had gone an extra ten minutes. "I didn't even notice."

He laughed at that. "I guess you still like school as much as you did back then, huh?"

"I guess so."

"Well, thanks to Ms. Smelding, I've already lost a third of my time with you tonight, right? If I stick to that half hour promise." He tilted his head, waiting for her response, and Jessica had to swallow to help herself speak. Something about being this close to him, and looking into those eyes that were identical to Nathan's, rendered her nearly speechless.

She finally managed, "I just want to make sure I'm back in time to see Nathan before he goes to sleep. Another ten minutes should be okay."

He smiled, dimples and all. "Good to know."

Ms. Smelding exited the classroom and paused to look at them. She seemed to assess the fact that he had been waiting on Jessica, then pursed her lips for a moment before speaking. "Mr. Martin, isn't it?" she said to Chad.

"Yes, ma'am."

"Met you at the staff meetings. Biology."

It was more a statement than a question, but Chad nodded. "Yes, ma'am."

"You know, I started teaching here when I was about your age. I was the youngest staff member at Stockville back then, like you." She smiled and bobbed her silver head as though remembering those days. "It's a small campus, I know, but it grows on you. Kind of like a small town. There's something nice about everyone knowing everyone." She glanced at Jessica and added, "And every now and then, you find one or two who really appreciate your effort. Makes it all worthwhile."

"Yes, ma'am," Chad repeated, smiling at the woman and then at Jess.

"You two have a good night," she said, still bobbing her head as she walked away.

"I think I just lost five more minutes of coffee time while we were talking to Ms. Smelding," Chad said. "Come on, let's go." He began walking, and Jess noticed he still took the long, even strides that he'd had in high school, and like back then, she had to increase her pace to keep up. When he reached the stairs, he noticed the fact and laughed.

"Habit. I never learned to slow down."

"Not a problem," she said. "I can still keep up. I'm used to chasing after Nathan."

While they continued down the stairs, he said, "Lainey's only been mobile for about six months, but I feel the same way. And it's like I need eyes in the back of my head. You should have seen her at Christmas. One minute she was sitting by the tree, sweetest little girl on the planet, then I turned my back for a moment to grab the camera and half of the presents were unwrapped."

Jessica laughed. "Nathan did the same thing when he was two. That was a fun Christmas, waiting to see what he was going to get into next."

"She's eighteen months," he said and opened the door for her to exit the English building.

A blast of cold air hit them, and she squinted against the chill. "Goodness."

"Yeah, I'm sure you remember that you never know what you're going to get here, weatherwise. It's supposed to warm up by the end of the week, if the forecast is right, though it's hard to imagine that now," he said. "Let's get to the coffee shop where it's warm."

"Which way?" she asked, following beside him down the front steps of the building and toward the quad.

"Not far, but more than a walk. We'll need to drive. You want to follow me?" he asked, moving briskly toward the parking lot.

"Sure." Jessica was reminded again of how long his legs were, but she didn't mind that they were moving quicker now, since she was anxious to get out of the chilly air. She kept up with him without problem.

"I'm here," he said, indicating an older-model silver BMW, parked in the row reserved for staff. "Where are you parked?"

"Right there," she said, moving quickly to her Ford Escort, opening the door and climbing in, before she realized that he hadn't gotten in his car but had followed her and was attempting to open her door. She nearly knocked him down when she flung the car door open.

"You're making it difficult for me to be a gentleman," he said with a grin.

She laughed and dropped her stack of books on the passenger seat. "Sorry, I guess I'm used to opening the door for myself now."

"You shouldn't be." He paused, as if he was going to say more, but then indicated his car. "I'll lead."

Jessica cranked her car, and a frigid blast of air pushed through the vents before she had the wherewithal to turn on the heat and wait for the car to warm up.

You shouldn't be.

Her heart thumped in her chest. She hadn't even realized how much she'd missed having someone care for her enough to open her door. She hadn't really realized how much she'd missed having someone like Chad.

After following him a couple of blocks, she pulled her car into the parking space beside his BMW. She took in the red-and-white striped awning of the coffee shop, the white iron tables that lined the front porch and the checked curtains adorning the windows. Several couples and groups of college-age kids sat throughout the cozy interior, and Jessica immediately knew why Chad had thought of this spot for their meeting. It was casual, yet intimate and a place that would be conducive to old friends getting reacquainted.

Was this the place where she would tell him about Nathan?

She closed her eyes. *God, if I'm supposed to tell him tonight, help me to find the right words. And if it isn't the right time, help me to know that, too.*

Her car door opened, and she instantly jumped. Then she turned to find Chad standing there waiting for her to climb out.

"I could get used to this, you know," she said.

He guided her toward the entrance of the coffee shop and opened that door, too. "Would that be such a bad thing?" he asked as she passed through the doorway.

"No, I don't suppose it would."

The entrance was narrow, causing her to brush against him as she went through. And she instantly realized that there wasn't anything that could warm you up quicker than human contact.

A sign inside the door proclaimed the night Art Night, and Jessica noticed a couple of easels were actually set up in cozy corners of the café and that the artists, possibly some of the art students from the school, were painting on canvases while patrons sipped coffee and admired the local talent.

"Hello, Mr. Martin," a group of kids called from a table in the corner.

Chad returned the greeting and then made his way to a welcoming alcove on one side of the shop, where a wide bookshelf housed a bounty of eclectic titles and a comfy couch bordered by fringed antique lamps gave the impression of privacy within the public café.

"This okay?" he asked, motioning toward the burgundy sofa. He moved a couple of beaded floral pillows out of the way so she could sit down.

"Yes, very nice," she said, taking in the assortment of coffee-themed paintings adorning the red brick wall. She looked at the small name at the corner of the paintings and wondered if the artist, Gina Brown, was actually here, painting while they chatted. "I love the art night theme."

"That's one of the things I like most about coming here, the atmosphere. They promote local artists, musicians, singers. It makes every visit here unique, something special."

Jessica immediately felt special, just being here with Chad.

A waitress came over. Like the other waitresses and waiters, she wore black from head to toe and had her hair pulled into a low, classic ponytail. "Hello, Mr. Martin, I've got my biology homework ready for class tomorrow morning," she said.

"That's good," Chad said, "but I didn't come here to check up on my students. We really are here for the coffee."

The girl smiled. "Sorry. Just thought I should let you know." She withdrew a small pad and a pencil from her pants pocket. "So, what would you like this evening?"

"What do you want?" he asked Jess.

"Just coffee."

"Regular or decaf?" the waitress asked, but Chad intervened.

"Just coffee?" he asked. "Don't you want to try something a little more special?"

Jessica laughed. She really hadn't gotten into all of the fancy coffee drinks, since her grandmother's farm in Tennessee had been about as rural as you get and much less modern than Claremont or Stockville. Even though they were small towns, the quaint coffee shop proved they'd kept up with the times. And Jessica was still catching up. "What do you suggest?"

Chad scanned the list of specialty drinks scrawled in fluorescent chalk on a neon-trimmed standing blackboard. "How about the white chocolate mocha?"

"Okay, I'm game," Jessica said to the waitress.

"And for you, Mr. Martin?"

"Just coffee, regular, please."

The waitress nodded and left to retrieve their order while Jessica gaped.

"I thought you said I should get something more special than regular coffee."

He smiled. "Because I think you'll like it. Not me, though. I'm a regular coffee kind of guy."

"And how do you know I'm not a regular coffee kind of girl?" she asked, as the waitress put two oversize mugs on a tray and headed back to the alcove.

"Because," he said simply. "You're special."

Jessica could feel her cheeks heating and tried to figure out the best response for his flattering statement, but Chad saved her from the task when he continued talking.

"So, I figure we have about fifteen to twenty minutes left if you're wanting to get back home in time to tuck your little guy in." He lifted a shoulder. "I'm afraid Lainey goes to bed too early on my late class nights for me to get a chance to tuck her in, so I'll just have to make tomorrow night's good night hug extra special."

"Where does she go when you're teaching late?" Jess asked and wondered if she was about to learn that his ex-wife was still local.

"My mom comes over on Tuesday and Thursday evenings and takes care of her. It's a good deal all the way around. Mom wants more time with her, and I have to work late two nights per week." He paused to accept his coffee from the waitress then waited while Jessica got hers. "What about your son? I'm assuming he's with your folks while you're here."

Jessica sipped the hot drink, which was amazingly rich and sweet, then answered, "Yes, he stays with them.

Of course, that's pretty easy since I'm still living there for the time being."

"You said his name is Nathan?" Chad asked, and she could tell he was working hard to make this conversation seem normal, instead of what it was, more of a joint interrogation. They both were dying to know everything about what was going on in the other's world, and there was way too much to catch up on than could be handled in a mere fifteen minutes.

"Yes, it's Nathan. It means 'God has given,'" she said, then added, "but I didn't know that until this past Sunday, when Brother Henry told us at church."

He sipped his coffee. "I saw Brother Henry there a couple of weeks ago."

"You did?" Chad had never been a churchgoer growing up, not until he met Jessica and that became one of the ways he could see her more often. She'd hoped the visits to the church had an impact, but she wasn't certain that he'd kept it up after she left.

He laughed. "Don't look too shocked. I'm not a regular, but I've actually been back a few times since high school, usually around New Years each year. You know, resolutions and all. I made the same one this year, which was why I went back Sunday before last. But this time it's different. I'm more interested in going back regularly again."

"Why is it different now?"

He looked thoughtful, his mouth crooking to one side as he formed his answer.

Jessica waited, sipped more coffee. Maybe this wasn't something he wanted to share with her. Maybe they weren't as close as she thought or time had destroyed the closeness they once shared. "You don't have to tell me."

"It isn't that. I'm just trying to think of the best way to explain it." He paused, then said with a shrug, "Things change once you have kids, don't you think? You start looking at the big picture, at the future and all. And I suppose you hope things will be a little better for your child. You want to do whatever you can to make life a little easier on them, right?"

She nodded, understanding exactly what he meant.

"Because of Lainey, I want to stick to the resolution this time. I want her to grow up going to church. My mom stopped after my dad left, so Becky and I didn't get the chance to go. Then when I got old enough to drive myself, it didn't really seem like something I wanted to do." He took another sip of coffee. "Until I met you."

"I think it's good for kids to grow up in church. They need to know that there's someone always in their corner and that He understands life is tough and they're going to make mistakes. They need to know that even when no one else seems to, that He understands." Jessica didn't know how she'd have made it through that lonely time when she left Claremont if she hadn't had her faith. She'd missed Chad, her parents, her home. But God hadn't left her then, and he'd given her Nathan, the beautiful baby who truly had been sent from God.

Then she recalled how often she'd talked to Chad about her faith back in high school, when she wanted him to come to church with her. She'd thought that was what was missing in his life, and she'd wanted his world to be better. He'd been dealt a rough road, with his father running out on them when Chad had barely started school. His mother, Chad and Becky had struggled financially, and they'd struggled spiritually. So consequently, a lot of her conversations with him back then had involved her beliefs.

Evidently, he remembered.

"We promised each other that our kids would go to church," he said softly, as though he wanted to make sure none of his students were eavesdropping on this part of their conversation.

"Yes, we did," she said, remembering those quiet conversations they'd shared when they'd thought they were planning their future. Before that night when she'd learned about his scholarship and left him to have their son.

"I didn't make it to the church last Sunday. Mom woke up with a stomach virus, and I went over there to take care of her. But I saw your folks there Sunday before last, when Lainey and I went."

Jessica recalled her mother's thorough examination of the auditorium after Brother Henry's sermon and now realized who she'd been hoping to see.

"I asked them how you were, and they told me you were doing fine, but they didn't say you were moving home. And they didn't mention that you'd had a son."

Jessica knew why they hadn't said anything. She'd told them she'd tell Chad herself, in her own time, when she believed the timing was right. Thankfully, they'd respected her wishes.

"Mom always said she wouldn't turn a deaf ear to gossip, but she'd do her best not to be the one starting it," Jessica said with a laugh, and she hoped that explanation would fly. "Maybe she's holding true to that."

"I guess she is," he agreed. "So, how old is Nathan?"

Her pulse quickened. "He's five, in kindergarten at

Claremont Elementary," she said. "He likes school, I think, but I was a little nervous about him changing schools in the middle of the school year. Even though it's kindergarten and the curriculum is probably fairly similar from one school system to the next, I didn't know how it would affect him to be uprooted in the middle of his first year. Didn't know how he'd feel leaving his friends in Tennessee and being faced with the challenge of making new friends and all."

Her words came out rapid because she was praying he wasn't trying to determine exactly when she'd become pregnant. Nathan was actually closer to six now than five, but she wouldn't explain that now. Not until she decided whether she'd be telling Chad about him tonight.

And something about this place, the coffee shop, with several of his students around, made it seem like the wrong place for sharing that news. They needed to be alone, completely alone. Or maybe with Nathan. Maybe if she had Nathan with her, telling Chad would be a little easier. Or at least make it harder for him to become openly upset.

"Jessica?" he asked, and she realized that she'd been so lost in her thoughts that she hadn't heard whatever he'd just said.

"Sorry. I'm afraid my mind was wandering for a second there." She cleared her throat, sipped more of the deliciously sweet, warm drink and asked, "What did you say?"

"I asked about Nathan's father."

She honestly felt the color drain from her face. Maybe she wasn't going to have a choice about when she told him after all. "What about his father?"

"I asked why you didn't marry him." He took another swallow of coffee, tilted his head apologetically. "Listen, you don't have to tell me, but I've never held back when I wanted to know something. You know that. And specifically, I never held back when I wanted to know something from you. We were close, Jess, close enough that I know if you didn't marry the guy who fathered your child, there must have been something wrong. What happened? What did he do? Why didn't you marry him?"

She steadied her hands around the mug, took it to her lips and made herself drink. *God, help me get this right. I don't want to lie to him, but I just can't tell him tonight.* "I didn't marry him...because he never asked."

Chad's eyes widened, and the deep forest-green seemed to darken even more as he absorbed her response. She knew that wasn't the answer he'd been expecting, but it was the truth, even if the only reason he hadn't asked was because she never gave him the chance.

"You loved him, though?" Chad continued.

An easy question, an easy answer. "With all my heart."

I still do.

His mouth tightened, and Jessica was mentally prepared to tell him everything. Apparently tonight was the night to get it all out in the open and to hope that he could forgive her.

She took a calming breath then slowly let it out.

"Okay," he said, before she could start. "Okay. I know this is probably not the smartest thing I've ever done but it's the only way I know how to be."

She blinked, set her mug on the table. She hadn't even noticed the ceiling fan above them earlier, but its gentle breeze was suddenly too cold. Chilling her to the bone.

Or was that her nerves getting the best of her? "What do you mean?" she asked.

"Honest. That's the way I am, and I'm just going to lay it all out." He placed his mug next to hers and moved a little closer to her on the couch. Then he tenderly placed his fingertips against her cheek and pushed a wayward lock of hair away from her face. "Listen, Jess, I know I'm the reason you left back then." He glanced around, apparently making sure no one was close enough to hear his next words. "I know that it was because of what happened between us that you felt you couldn't stay around."

The room grew blurry around him. Jessica was so focused on his face, on his eyes and on his misconception of what happened back then. She barely heard the low rumble of voices from the groups at the other tables, hardly noticed the frosty breeze from the fan. Yes, she left because of what happened between them but not for the reason he thought. And here he was, being honest with her, when she'd started it all with that lie. "Chad, no, that's not…"

He held up a hand, then he took his palm to her hand and squeezed it softly. Warmth rippled through her from his compassionate touch. "Hear me out. I know that things went wrong for us back then, that you couldn't forgive yourself or me for what happened that night. And I understand that after you left Alabama—after you left me—you eventually met someone else, fell in love and had a child. I don't know what happened that caused him not to want to marry you. In fact, I'd have to say that the guy is a fool."

"He's not. Chad, if I would have just told—" she started, but again, he shook his head and halted her words.

"I don't want to hear about him," he said. "Really, I don't. Ever. I don't want to know anything about anyone who left you, anyone who hurt you in any way. The thought of you being alone with your baby—" he shook his head "—Jess, I want you to know that in spite of the fact that I did love my wife when I married her, the truth is that you were my first true love, and you always will be. Back then, I wanted to be with you forever, and when you left, all I could think about was finding you and proving to you that I could really wait for you for as long as it took."

Jessica's mouth trembled, and the back of her throat pinched tight, anticipating oncoming tears. "Chad, I'm sorry about leaving the way I did."

He sighed. "I drove to your house every day for an entire month after you left. Becky went with me. Your parents said you'd left and that you didn't want to see anyone, didn't want to talk to anyone."

Because Jessica had told them that, and she'd meant it. But her parents hadn't told her that Chad had come over. Then again, she'd asked them not to mention him to her because it hurt so much to know she'd left the father of her child. That she'd left the one she loved. Now she wished she hadn't been so adamant about that request. She didn't realize that he'd tried so hard to find her. "I didn't know," she whispered.

"I even drove to Tennessee," he said softly. "But I didn't really know where to go. All Becky knew was that your grandmother lived in the mountains in the northern part of the state." He smiled. "Tennessee is a big state, and believe it or not, there are more than seventy women named Pearl Bowman who live there."

Jessica's chest clenched, her heart aching for what she'd put him through back then. She had no idea what he'd gone through to find her. "Chad, I had no idea."

"But I never found you, and we both went in different directions," he said.

"Can I get you anything else? Or are you ready for your check?" the waitress said, and Jessica jumped. She hadn't even heard her approach, and from the look on Chad's face, neither had he.

He glanced at his watch. "I've kept you too long," he said. Then he said to the waitress, "the check please."

The girl fished the check from her pocket, handed it over to Chad and then looked at Jessica, making her wonder just how much she'd heard.

But Chad no longer seemed to care and was focused, again, solely on Jessica. He took her hands in his, looked at her with those intense green-gold eyes.

"I can't believe that we weren't meant to run into each other on campus the other night," he said.

"I know. I've thought the same thing."

"I understand that you love your son's father, that you always will. There's a bond there that won't be broken. I do understand that because of what I have with Lainey. No, things could never work out between myself and Kate, but I will always care about her, if for no other reason than the fact that she's Lainey's mother. But if you aren't going to be with his father, and if you're willing to try at another relationship," he said, then audibly took a deep breath and continued, "then I want you to try—with me."

Jessica's world seemed to tilt off balance. Chad wanted a relationship with her, and she truly wanted one with him. But he didn't know the truth about Nathan, and she still couldn't gather the courage to tell him. "I don't know what to say," she whispered.

"Just say yes." His smile made the situation seem less dismal, especially when that perfect dimple flashed, and she couldn't help but picture that very same smile, the very same dimple…on their son.

"Yes."

Chapter Five

Jessica entered the day care center Wednesday morning with Chad's words still echoing through her mind.

"If you're willing to try at another relationship, then I want you to try—with me."

He'd made the statement, then paid for their coffees and walked her to the car. There was a moment of awkwardness where he opened her door, leaned in and told her good-night. Jessica thought he might kiss her, but Chad surprised her, placing his fingertips against her cheek before gently brushing them down her face. Then he'd told her he would call her today so they could plan a real date.

Thankfully, they'd remembered to exchange cell numbers, and she'd already received a text message from him this morning.

I'm glad you said yes.

She couldn't stop smiling, and her coworker noticed.

"Okay, what's his name, and does he have a brother?" Angie, the toddler room teacher, asked.

Jessica completed her current task of straightening

the tiny jackets hanging along the wall hooks, ran her palm over a fuzzy pink pom-pom that embellished one of the little hoods and laughed. "Am I that obvious?"

"You've met someone, and from the look on your face, he's made quite an impression." Angie moved around a table filled with toddlers, their faces expectant as they waited for her to distribute their morning snack. She handed each of the tykes a muffin, then nodded toward the sippy cups. "Can you start those?"

"Sure," Jessica said, and followed behind Angie to hand out the apple juice.

"I thought you'd just moved back here," Angie said, grinning as she gently steered one little boy's hands back to his own muffin, since he appeared to be making more of an effort to pick the blueberries off of his neighbor's food than to eat his own.

"I did." Jessica helped one of the little girls break her muffin into manageable pieces. She'd wrinkled her nose at hers and was more interested in poking her fingers at the blueberries than consuming any.

"So how did you meet a Mr. Wonderful so quickly? I mean, Claremont doesn't have an abundance of party places or social hangouts for people our age."

Angie was probably ten years older than Jessica, but Jess understood what she meant.

"I'd known him before I left," she said and couldn't hold back an even bigger smile as she thought of Chad, their past relationship and the one they were starting now.

"Well, it looks like you two are catching up rather nicely." Angie placed the extra muffins in a Tupperware container and stored them in the wooden pantry.

"Yeah, we are."

The children in the class one by one finished their snacks, and Angie and Jess wiped their crumb-covered mouths before helping them move from the eating area to the play centers.

Jessica was considered a "floater," or someone who rotated from room to room depending on which teacher needed help on a particular day. She'd also been hired to substitute as a main teacher or assistant teacher when any of the others were out. Today she was filling in for Angie's assistant, who'd called in sick. Jess liked the opportunity to move from class to class; it meant she'd be working with all of the children at the center eventually.

She was particularly excited that she'd been assigned to the toddler room today. There was something so endearing about this precocious age, from eighteen months to two years. The energy in the room was palpable, and since she was already feeling positive from her time with Chad last night, this was an added treat to what promised to be an amazing week.

A tug at her jeans brought her attention to a tiny blonde girl, her big blue eyes looking up at Jess as she held up a book. "Peese," she said then smiled into her cheeks, so that Jessica got a full view of sweet little baby teeth lining her gums. She instantly thought of Nathan and that cute new gap that sometimes caused his *s*'s to slur.

Jess grinned and scooped the little girl into her arms, then took the book from her hand. "The Three Bears," she said. "Oh, that's a good one. Why don't we go over to the reading corner and see what happens."

She noticed that this child was one of the younger children in the class and quite petite, making her stand out from the others in the room. Then again, she stood out anyway, with those sky-blue eyes, constantly examining everything around her, and gentle blond curls that framed her face and made her look almost angelic.

"Tank oo," she said as Jessica sat on an oversize thick blue floor pillow with the girl in her lap. Several other toddlers, seeing that Jess was about to start a story, worked their way to the reading cove and gathered to sit on the smaller kid-size pillows.

Jess got excited about their natural desire to learn what happens in the story and enjoyed the way their eyes lit up as they examined the animals featured on the cover of the book.

"Oh, the three bears!" one boy, obviously one of the older children in the group, exclaimed and then plopped down on a red patchwork pillow to listen.

Angie let Jessica take over with the reading center while she filled out yellow identification stickers for each toddler and placed one on each child's back. "To help you learn their names," she mouthed to Jess, while Jessica read the story.

Another young girl with long red curls worked her way into Jessica's lap to sit opposite the tiny blonde. Both girls grinned at each other and took turns peering at the pages, while Jessica made sure each child sitting around them could also view what happened to Goldilocks as she progressed from bowl to bowl and bed to bed.

"Someone's been eating my porridge," Jessica said, lowering her voice to mimic the papa bear. She followed suit with the mama bear and baby bear, while all of the children giggled at her attempt at bear voices.

She then took the bears through the discovery of their chairs and then finally their beds.

"Someone's been sleeping in my bed, and she's still there!" Jessica squealed in her best baby bear voice.

Nathan loved for her to read stories to him before bed, and these children enjoyed this story just as much, particularly the two girls snuggling against her while she read. They clapped and laughed as Goldilocks went from one awkward predicament to another and squealed when she finally ran from the house with the bear family watching her go.

By the time the story was done, Angie had placed a name tag on each child's back except the two in Jessica's lap. Then she patted each of their backs to put their identification stickers in place. Jessica turned toward the red-haired girl, still grinning from the story and sending an adorable array of tiny freckles across her cheeks with her smile.

Jess glanced at her name tag, then said, "You liked that, didn't you, Blaire?"

"Yes!" Blaire said, clapping with enthusiasm while her red curls bounced against her shoulders. Then she climbed off Jessica's lap and ran to play with the puzzles.

"Looks like you picked a good story—" Jessica said, then glanced at the blonde girl's back to add her name to the statement.

Her breath caught in her throat.

What were the chances?

Then she repeated, "Looks like you picked a good story, Lainey."

She looked again at the cherubic girl. Blond hair, sky-blue eyes, sweet puckered lips. "Lainey," she repeated.

The toddler blinked and grinned, again showing all of those tiny teeth.

She seemed to be the right age for Chad's little girl, and she had the same name. A fairly unique name. But there was no hint of green or gold in her wide, round eyes. And her hair was baby fine, not wavy and thick like Chad's or Nathan's. Her mouth wasn't Chad's. Neither was her petite nose.

But still, the name was right, the age was right.

The tiny tot with *Lainey* on her back kissed Jess's cheek, gave her another endearing "Tank oo," and then scurried away to play with the other boys and girls at the puzzle center area.

"Angie?" Jessica asked.

"Yeah?"

"What's Lainey's last name?"

"Beautiful, isn't she?" Angie said, admiring the adorable girl, dressed in pink overalls, a lace-trimmed white undershirt and matching pink tennis shoes. She looked like a living doll, literally. "It's Martin. Lainey Mae Martin. I love the name, don't you? Modern and old fashioned all rolled together. I think I'm going to try to do something like that when I have children. And it suits her, don't you think? She's such a beautiful little girl and a sweetie. She only comes here a couple days a week, on Mondays and Wednesdays, but I really enjoy having her when she's here." She smiled at the little girl, her blond brows currently drawn together as she worked to put a chunky puzzle piece in the corresponding hole.

Lainey Mae. Mae was Chad's mother's name. "Chad's little girl," Jessica said, not really paying attention to the fact that she said it aloud.

Angie nodded. "You know him? Chad Martin? It's no wonder his daughter's gorgeous, huh? If I knew all college instructors would look like that, I'd sign back up right now. I mean, he's an incredibly nice-looking..." She paused. "Wait. Is that your Mr. Wonderful? Chad Martin?"

Was he *her* Mr. Wonderful? Jessica took only a second before responding the same way she had last night.

"Yes."

On Mondays and Wednesdays, Chad started his day early, dropping Lainey off at the day care center around 6:30 a.m. and then heading to Stockville to teach a 7:30 a.m. class. He'd planned his schedule so that his four classes ran pretty much back-to-back and finished at 2:30 p.m., allowing him to pick Lainey up by 3:00 p.m.

Last night he'd learned that, due to her work schedule, Jessica had started her classes every afternoon right after she got off at the day care center. So it'd be pretty much impossible to see her in the afternoon or perhaps have an outing where their kids could meet and play. He was very interested in introducing her to Lainey and even more interested in introducing Lainey to her son. If this relationship was going anywhere long term—and he definitely wanted it to—it was important for their kids to be receptive to the idea.

He smiled, thinking that merely a week ago he saw himself as a single parent and didn't see any chance of that changing in the near future. He'd dated a few women since his divorce, but he'd never met anyone that he wanted to introduce to Lainey. No one had made it past a second date, and he couldn't see any of them as a potential mother to his little girl.

With Jess, it wasn't a question of whether he wanted her to meet Lainey. It was simply a question of how soon he could arrange the meeting.

He pulled into the day care parking lot and noticed that the older kids, the four-year-olds, were out on the playground, giggling wildly and running nonstop. This was the first day in weeks that had been warm enough for them to play outside, and you could tell the kids appreciated the opportunity from their unbridled enthusiasm.

Chad wondered if the toddlers, Lainey's group, made the trip outdoors today. Lainey loved to play outside, but he didn't expect to see her out now. He knew the schedule for the toddler class called for an afternoon nap, and his little lady definitely still needed one each day. Often he'd arrive to pick her up just in time for her to reach for him and let him hold her while she blinked sleepy eyes and prepared for the remainder of her day.

If he didn't have so many papers to review and grade, he'd take her to the park this afternoon. She loved feeding the ducks. Chad nodded to himself, forming a playdate in his mind for Lainey and Jessica's son, Nathan. If the forecast for the week remained as predicted, Saturday was expected to hit sixty degrees, plenty warm enough for a trip to Hydrangea Park for him, Jessica and the kids.

The image set well in his mind.

He was planning on another casual coffee date for Thursday night, when the two of them ended their classes at the same time. Then, if all went as planned, he'd take Jessica out for their first real date Friday night. Dinner at Messina's then maybe a movie.

He punched in his parent code on the keypad by the day care door, entered the colorful lobby and signed the parent log. That was one of the things that sold him on this particular place for his daughter, the safety measures they took for the children. He didn't like leaving Lainey, but if he had to, he wanted to know she was in the best possible care. Although it was a bit more pricey than the other child care facilities around, this one was well worth the added expense. Lainey was happy here, and that made Chad happy, too.

He greeted the office manager and then headed across the open play area, where the three-year-olds were busy with afternoon exercises, jumping up and down in time with the Barney DVD playing on the television and laughing at their teacher, who was also jumping along and singing one of the popular Barney songs.

The teacher waved at Chad, and he returned the gesture.

He gently pushed open the door to the toddler room and saw the familiar illumination of stars and planets slowly circling the ceiling and walls from the sleep machine the teachers used during nap time. His last class today ended early, and he'd arrived at day care before nap time ended.

Blinking a few times to let his eyes adjust to the dimness within the room, Chad nearly didn't notice Angie, Lainey's teacher, moving toward him. Her whisper broke through the gentle hum of the sleep machine and the precious sounds of children sleeping.

"She's still napping," Angie said softly. "But you can hold her and help her wake up if you're ready for her to go."

Lainey was a fairly sound sleeper, and Chad knew he could scoop her up and take her to the car, put her in her car seat and let her finish out her nap on the ride home. "Thanks," he said, matching her whisper to keep from disturbing the sleeping children. He took a couple of steps to reach the long line of short cubbies where the children's jackets and backpacks were stored, grabbed Lainey's backpack and pink hooded jacket and then scanned the room for his little angel.

The toddlers had colorful cushioned nap mats that they used for sleeping, but some preferred the long pillows in the reading center and still others tended to find their way into a teacher's arms to slumber. That was Lainey's favorite spot, and Chad had been a little surprised to see she wasn't in Angie's arms. However, Dana, Angie's assistant, could have pulled cuddle duty this afternoon. He had a feeling her teachers enjoyed holding her while she slept almost as much as he did.

He searched the darkness for Dana or for a sign that Lainey had changed her usual routine and joined the others to sleep on the mats today.

"Dana is out sick today," Angie whispered. "But I believe Lainey has taken a liking to our new floating teacher." She indicated the far window, where slim fingers of sunlight filtered through the wooden blinds to outline a woman, sitting in a rocking chair with a child snuggled in her arms. "I think you may know her," Angie added quietly, then turned back toward her desk and left Chad to find his way through the sleeping palettes to the woman who held his daughter.

His eyes adjusting more to the dim room as he made his way to the other side, Chad's pulse quickened when the familiarity of the woman was too distinct to miss. Her shiny chocolate hair was pulled into a ponytail, the honey highlights capturing the sunlight as it fell across one shoulder. Her other shoulder formed a pillow for his daughter. Her mouth was near Lainey's forehead, and her arms cradled her as lovingly as if she were holding her own child. She rocked gently, while Lainey's mouth puckered around her balled up fist, her tiny thumb hooked within her lips.

"Jess," he whispered, and his heart melted at the sight of her holding his child.

She'd been watching him, he realized, as he crossed the room. While his eyes had been adjusting to the dimness, hers had been completely aware, and she'd apparently known that he was coming. Known that this was his little girl that she held in her arms.

"Hey," she whispered, so softly he had to move closer to hear. Then she shifted and eased herself up out of the rocker. "Do you want me to carry her to your car?"

He almost said yes, just so he could see Jessica holding Lainey a little longer, but then he thought better of her offer and edged closer, close enough to slide his arms under Lainey's back and shift her to his embrace. "I won't take you from your class," he whispered. Then he paused, his fingers brushing against Jessica's arms as they moved his sleeping girl.

"You have her?" she asked, before she slid her arms away, and he nodded.

"Jess," he said, and the emotion of the moment, of the rightness of it, caused words to fail him.

Jessica looked at him, her dark eyes peering into his, then she sighed as her gaze moved to Lainey, still sleeping in his arms. "You're right," she whispered an easy smile lighting up her face. "She is pretty amazing."

"Yes," he answered, just as quietly. "She is." And he wondered if she realized that he wasn't only talking about the angel in his arms.

Chapter Six

"I wonder whether Chad and Lainey will be at church tonight," Anna Bowman said, stirring a large pot of bubbling potato soup on the stove as she spoke.

Jessica donned a green oven mitt, removed the cast iron skillet from the oven and poured the sizzling grease into the cornbread batter. "I don't think so," she said, folding the hot oil into the mixture then pouring it all back into the skillet. "When he called me on my way home, he said that he had a ton of papers to grade, and when I mentioned that I was glad my Wednesday class schedule allowed me to go to the night service, he didn't say anything about coming." She returned the skillet to the oven and waited, knowing there was more on her mom's mind than whether Chad and Lainey would be at church tonight.

Her mother picked up the wooden pepper grinder and gave it several good twists, adding a healthy dose of black pepper to the soup. Then she tasted a spoonful and nodded her approval. "You know, Jess, I've been thinking about Chad and Nathan and everything. That boy looks quite a lot like his father. He's got your mouth and nose, but those eyes. Those are undeniably Martin eyes. Don't you think it'd be better to tell him the truth before he sees Nathan and figures it out for himself?"

Jessica had been thinking the same thing all afternoon, particularly after she'd spent so much time with Lainey. Seeing those baby blue eyes on Chad's daughter and knowing she must have inherited that feature from her mother made Jess realize how extremely unique Nathan's eyes are and how it'd be nearly impossible for his father not to notice. But thanks to her conversation with Chad during her drive home, she now knew that she had a couple of chances in the near future to tell him about their son. Even if she didn't know how he'd react to the news.

"Chad wants our children to meet and get to know each other, and he's invited Nathan and me to go to Hydrangea Park Saturday with him and Lainey."

Her mother stopped stirring and turned the heat down on the stove. Then she wiped her hands on a dish towel and leaned against the kitchen counter. "And what are you going to do about that? Surely you don't plan to show up Saturday with Nathan and introduce him as his son." She ran her teeth across her lower lip. "I'll admit that your father and I thought it'd be wonderful for Nathan to meet his father now, and we thought we were doing the right thing by asking you to come back here and getting you started at the college."

Jessica could hear the "but" coming, and sure enough, it did.

"But being around Nathan these past couple of weeks, well, I've seen how observant he is and how smart. I know Chad wouldn't do anything intentionally to hurt him, but Nathan won't miss a thing about that meeting, and I want to make sure he isn't the one who ends up being hurt by all of this." She fidgeted with the hand towel. "I just want everything to be perfect." She smiled softly. "I've been praying that you can give Nathan a real family—with his daddy."

"I've been praying the same thing," Jessica admitted. "And you know how I feel about Chad, how I've always felt about him."

"I know, honey," her mother said. "And that's why everything that happens between you two this week is so important. You should consider talking to Chad before Saturday, if at all possible, or postponing the trip to the park until you get a chance to have that conversation."

Jessica glanced out the kitchen window to make sure Nathan was still in the backyard. He was, laughing and cheering as his granddaddy pushed him on the tire swing. She didn't want him hearing this conversation. She planned to talk to him this week, too, about the possibility of meeting his daddy, but she wasn't quite ready for that conversation yet. However, she'd have to have it soon, very soon. Before Saturday, in fact. "I agree with you completely. And Chad asked me to have coffee with him tomorrow night after class, like we did on Tuesday, and he also asked me to dinner Friday night." She couldn't hold back a smile.

"So..." her mother prompted.

"So, either tomorrow or Friday, I'll tell him about Nathan. I don't know which, but I'm hoping I'll know whenever the time is right." She fought the tug of apprehension pulling at her heart. "And I pray that everything goes well, that he'll love Nathan instantly and that he'll forgive me."

Her mother turned, peered out the window at the

picture-perfect scene in the backyard. The sky was growing dark, and apparently the guys had noticed. Nathan wiggled out of the swing and nearly lost his jacket in the process; then he fell into his granddaddy's arms. Jessica's father laughed and tugged the small denim coat back up his arms. Then he kissed Nathan's forehead and turned toward the back door.

"I don't know why I can't seem to stop worrying. Chad will love Nathan," her mother said quietly. "How could he not?"

"I know he will," Jessica agreed.

But will he love me?

Nathan, as usual, was a bundle of energy when he came in from playing, and the family chatted freely through dinner, but Jessica could barely make out the conversation. And the potato soup was delicious, she assumed, since her mother was an excellent cook, but she didn't taste a thing. On the contrary, her mind couldn't concentrate on any words spoken or any food eaten. Instead, she churned over the fact that she'd be sharing her secret with Chad before the week ended.

By the time they'd finished dinner and started the drive to church, Jessica's stomach was knotted and her head pounded relentlessly. She started pondering what would happen if they showed up at the church and found that Chad was there, that he'd finished his papers and decided to go.

It was the first time in her life that she actually hoped someone she cared about wouldn't attend church. How awful was that?

God, help me. I have to tell Chad before he sees Nathan. And I have to get over this fear of what he'll feel toward me because of what I've done. Dear God, if it be Your will, help me to find the courage to tell him. And help him to understand and forgive me. And I know this is a selfish plea, God, but if at all possible, help us to be a family, a real family. For Nathan and Lainey—and me.

Often, especially since she had Nathan and had been working full-time, Jessica found herself tired in the middle of the week and not overly eager to attend the midweek Bible study. In fact, when she first moved to Tennessee, she'd gone several months being content to attend the Sunday morning service and letting that suffice for her weekly spiritual nourishment.

Then, as the baby inside her stomach began to move and she realized that the precious life was certainly a gift from God, she decided that she needed more, she wanted more. God hadn't turned his back on her, but she had attempted to slowly turn her back on Him. And she needed Him then, while she was away from her parents and away from Chad, more than ever.

She'd gone back to church on Sunday evenings and then also added the midweek Bible study to her regular weekly schedule. And even though she was often tired from the pregnancy and from the hours she put in at the Tennessee day care, she learned that the Wednesday class gave her that something that was missing in her daily routine. Faith that things were going to get better and assurance that God would see her through. She simply needed more than a once-a-week acknowledgment of her faith and that midweek service gave her the push she needed to get through the remainder of the week.

She'd rarely missed a Wednesday service since, and she was uplifted at each and every one. Tonight the auditorium class taught by Brother Henry was perfect, focusing on drawing nearer to God and having full assurance of faith. The main point was to leave our troubles to God and be assured that He will respond and act in the way that is best for us. She underlined the key verse, Hebrews 10:22, in her Bible and decided that Scripture would be her guidance for this week and specifically for the moment when she told Chad the truth.

Near the end of the lesson, Brother Henry dismissed the parents of young children early so they could pick up their kids from class. She exited the auditorium with the other parents, many of them couples walking hand in hand toward the classroom halls, and found that being a single parent seemed a little more pronounced at her church. It wasn't as though anyone was making her feel out of place, though she did notice a few of the women she'd seen whispering in the lobby Sunday glance her way as she left the auditorium. It was more that it seemed she should have a man beside her here, maybe because every dream she'd had as a little girl of coming back to her home church and raising her family had involved not only herself and her children but a man who loved God as much as she...and a man who loved her.

She watched a young couple who appeared to be her age, mid-twenties, pick up their daughter from the toddler class, and she immediately thought of Lainey. Jess had bonded with the little girl today, even before she realized that Lainey was Chad's daughter. Jess noticed that classroom had a fish theme, with fish swimming in blue construction paper waves on the door and a fish net hanging from the ceiling in one corner of the room. The teacher at the door handed a boat made of craft sticks to the parents and explained that their daughter had learned about Peter, James and John fishing with Jesus.

Jess admired the tiny boat as she passed. She wouldn't have known it was a boat if the teacher hadn't said so. Basically, it was three craft sticks held together with an abundance of blue glue, but that was part of what made it so adorable. The teacher beamed at the little girl, proudly pointing at the boat she'd made for the Bible fishermen.

That would be the class Lainey would attend when she came to church, and that would be the class where Jessica and Chad would pick her up if they all came together.

A glimmer of hope flickered through her at that happy image. What if, after she told him, *that* was the type of vision Chad saw, too? What if those dreams, those childhood fantasies of the perfect family, would actually come true soon? And, with Lainey added to the picture, she'd actually have two children to pick up from Bible class.

She entered Nathan's classroom smiling and believing that everything might work out after all. She even felt a little eager about telling Chad the truth in the next couple of days and then spending Saturday together, all four of them, as a family.

A real, complete family.

"Hey, Jessica."

Jessica's father had dropped Nathan off at class earlier, so she hadn't seen his Wednesday night teacher. Now a petite girl with a light pink dress and mint cable sweater smiled at Jessica as though they were old friends. She wore a light green floppy hat embellished with a crocheted rose that perfectly matched the color combination of her dress and sweater. And she'd added dainty ballet slipper shoes that also pulled everything together in a sweet, simple look.

But Jessica couldn't place the pale, tiny girl.

"I'm sorry, I'm afraid I don't remember..." Jessica started, but then the girl's brown eyes lifted with her smile, and Jess recognized Hannah Taylor, who had been just a year younger than her in school. They'd gone to church together their entire lives. Hannah had been very athletic at Claremont High, cheering and running track. Back then, she'd been more toned, less frail. And not nearly as pale. She also had shiny brown hair that fell in gorgeous waves to her waist. Jessica had always admired Hannah's long hair. Now, Jess realized, her hair was gone. And she suddenly noticed the porcelain pink ribbon pin attached to the top of her sweater.

"You remember me now." She hadn't missed the signs of recognition on Jessica's face.

"Hannah," she said, controlling the emotion swelling in her heart. Her mind drifted back to middle school and the memorial service at the church for Hannah's mother after she lost her battle with breast cancer. And she also remembered that when she left Claremont, Hannah's sister had also been diagnosed with the disease. She didn't want to ask about Hannah's sister. She was afraid of the answer.

"It's okay," Hannah said, again smiling, which brought attention to the cheekbones that were a bit more accentuated than they'd been when Jess had last seen her six years ago. "I've changed a bit since you left town."

Jessica blinked to keep tears from pressing forward. Was she in remission? Or was she beyond that? And how did you go about asking?

"I'm Nathan's regular Wednesday night teacher,"

Hannah said. "I've been out the past few weeks, so I had a substitute filling in." Her shoulders rose in a subtle shrug. "I have good days and bad days, but I really try to get here when I can. It helps being with the kids." She took her attention from Jessica to a couple who'd entered the classroom behind her. "Jeremy, your mom and dad are here," Hannah said, and a black-haired little boy working on a Noah's ark puzzle with Nathan and a few other children looked up and then ran for the door. Hannah gave Jeremy's parents a brief update on how he did in class, handed them his take-home papers and then returned her attention to Jessica. "Don't look so sad. I'm actually doing a little better, and I'm going to a new doctor next week. He's supposed to be one of the best around."

"I'll pray that he'll be the perfect doctor for you," Jessica said, and Hannah smiled.

"I'd appreciate that." She looked toward Nathan, still busily working on the puzzle. His brows were drawn in concentration as he rotated a piece until it fell into place and formed one of two fat gray elephants within the oversize boat.

"Yes!" he exclaimed and then picked up another piece and drew his brows back together again.

"Nathan is a sweet little boy," Hannah said. "You know, I didn't even realize you had a son until your dad brought him to class tonight."

"Well, I had him after I left Claremont," Jess explained, but she knew when Hannah looked back at her that she suspected there was more to the story.

"I guess maybe it's because of the cancer or maybe from losing my mom as quickly as I did but I tend to notice things more clearly than I did before. My sister and I have been discussing that a lot lately, since we're both going through this together." She moistened her lips, sighed and then smiled at one of the children who'd pointed out how well they were doing on the puzzle. "Good job," she said to the boy, then continued to Jessica. "It's kind of like we're making sure we don't miss anything because we realize you never know how much time you have or when you may see someone for the last time." She paused and looked at Jess. "You understand?"

Jessica swallowed. "I think so."

"Anyway, now I'm a big believer that if you need to do something, or say something to someone, then you shouldn't waste time," Hannah said, as another set of parents entered the room, thanked her for teaching their daughter and then took their little girl.

There were three children remaining: a set of twin boys and Nathan. The three were obviously determined to complete the puzzle before they had to leave, and Jess wasn't about to take Nathan right now. She wanted to hear more of what Hannah would say, and she wanted to talk to her, to tell someone about what she was about to do, about how *she* needed to say something to someone and about how she'd been wasting time.

"Hannah," she started. Then the father of the twins poked his head in the door and called, "Matthew, Daniel, let's go."

"Bye, Nathan," they both chimed and followed their dad out of the room.

"Bye!" Nathan yelled. Then he asked, "Hey, Mom, I'm nearly done. Can I finish?"

"Sure," Jessica said. "If that's okay with your teacher."

"Of course," Hannah said. "I need to straighten up

in here before I leave." She moved to a table covered with crayons and started placing them in square plastic baskets.

"I'll help you." Jessica helped collect the crayons and pencils that littered the kid-size tables in the room.

"Our Bible lessons this quarter are covering families in the Bible," Hannah said. "Tonight we learned about Abraham and Sarah."

"And baby Isaac," Nathan chimed in from the puzzle table.

"That's right," Hannah said. "Good job remembering, Nathan."

He looked up from the puzzle and told Jessica, "They were really, really, really old when they had a baby."

Jessica laughed. "They sure were."

"Like, he was a million or something," Nathan said.

"More like a hundred," Jess clarified.

"But God helped them have a baby anyway, because He can do whatever He wants," Nathan said, the last *s* dragging out in a lisp.

"That's right," Hannah said. "He can."

"Nathan loves learning," Jessica said.

"I can tell." Hannah's hands paused as she picked up a pink crayon. "You know, he reminds me of someone."

"He does?" Jessica examined her little boy and knew that Hannah had probably put the pieces together. Had anyone else in town? Had anyone else at church?

"Did you know Chad Martin moved back to town, too, not long ago? He's got a little girl now." Hannah's voice was very soft, low and protective.

"I know," Jessica said, looking toward the door. No one was there, but she still kept her eyes focused on the opening to the hall. She didn't want anyone hearing

Chad's name associated with Nathan—not until she'd told him.

Hannah put the crayon in the basket Jessica held, then laid her palm on Jessica's wrist, causing Jess to look back at Nathan's young teacher.

"I always thought the two of you would get married. I think everyone did. And then you left, and then he married someone else."

"I know," Jessica repeated. So much had happened in the six years since she'd left. Hannah didn't look anything like the girl Jess knew in high school, the one who was the picture of health. Moreover, like her sister, she now had the disease that killed her mother. And Jessica had left the father of her son behind, and while she was gone, he'd met and married someone else.

"But he isn't married now," Hannah continued. "I don't know what happened, but from what I hear, he was hurt when it ended. The talk from the town gossips is that his wife treated him very badly and that he has custody of their daughter. She didn't try to keep her and doesn't even come to see her. But I've seen him with that little girl, and he's terrific with her."

Jessica didn't know about the rumors, though she suspected that Chad would tell her when he was ready to share that part of his life. But she knew one of Hannah's statements was true. He is very good with her.

"He's a good man," Hannah said. "He deserves to be happy, and so do you."

Jessica's mouth rolled inward, throat pinched.

"You should tell him," Hannah said softly. "About Nathan." She paused, apparently waiting for Jess to say something. When she didn't, Hannah continued, "He doesn't know, does he?"

There was no use denying the truth. Jessica shook her head. "Not yet."

"Don't wait too long," Hannah pleaded. "Remember, I'm a big believer that you shouldn't waste time."

"I won't," Jess said.

Her parents suddenly appeared at the door, both of them smiling as they saw Nathan pop the last piece of the puzzle into place and exclaim, "I did it!"

"You certainly did," his granddaddy said. "And now I see why we've been standing in the lobby and waiting for so long. I'm betting you had to finish the puzzle before you were ready to go, huh?"

"Yep," Nathan said, splaying his arms to show off his work. "What do you think, MeMaw?"

"It's absolutely amazing. Love all of those animals."

"Me, too," Nathan said. "But I bet that boat smelled yucky." He grabbed his take-home papers from a nearby table.

"Thank Ms. Hannah for teaching you," Jessica's mother instructed.

"Thanks!" Nathan said excitedly.

"You're welcome," she said as Nathan moved to the door.

"You coming, Mama?" he asked.

"Be right there," Jessica said. She let them start down the hall, out of earshot, then said, "I want to thank you, too. I needed a little encouragement, and you've given me that. I plan to tell him the truth this week."

"Well then, you say those prayers for me, and I'll say some for you. We'll call it even."

"You sure you're still a year younger than me? You've

got a lot of wisdom for someone who's only twenty-two," Jessica said with a grin.

"Cancer ages you quick," Hannah admitted, "but it's not always a good thing. Coming here, to church, helps my disposition most days, but I have to admit that sometimes I get a little mad at God. Then, when things get really bad, He's the one who gets me through, and I come back around. It's kind of hard to explain."

"I think you explained it great," Jessica said, then hugged Hannah before turning to go.

"One more thing," Hannah said.

Jess stopped at the door. "Yeah?"

"Ask Nathan to show you his paper from tonight. It touched my heart, and I think it'll touch yours, too. He—well, he really wants to know his daddy."

Jessica swallowed thickly and wondered what Nathan had put on that paper. "I know he does. And he will, soon."

"And something else," Hannah said.

"What?"

"He looks like him. I mean, I wouldn't have known so quickly if I hadn't known he was your son and hadn't remembered how close you and Chad were, but knowing that and then looking at Nathan…it was pretty easy to tell." She smiled. "That isn't a bad thing, at all, but I thought you should know."

"Have you heard anyone else say anything?" Jessica felt dread trying to creep its way into the joy of knowing Nathan looked like Chad.

Had anyone else noticed?

"No, but I'll let you know if I do. Then again, after this week, that won't matter, will it? He's going to meet his son."

"Yes, he is." She waved and left the classroom feeling better that Hannah hadn't heard any suspicions about Nathan's paternity from anyone else in town. Maybe she'd be able to tell Chad before he learned it from someone else.

She made her way to the lobby, where the only people remaining were her parents, Nathan and Brother Henry, apparently waiting on all of them to leave so he could lock up.

"Sorry," she said. "I was visiting with Hannah Taylor."

"No problem at all," Brother Henry said. "She's a sweet girl, isn't she, and bless her heart, she's been through quite a lot."

"Yes, she has," Jess said, while her parents nodded in agreement.

"I'm feeling better tonight, though," Hannah said, rounding the corner with her teacher's tote on her arm. She was so small now that the bag seemed to swallow her side. "Because I had a terrific group of kids in my class."

"She had me!" Nathan said. "Bye, Ms. Hannah."

"Bye, Nathan," Hannah said with a smile. She added a goodbye to Brother Henry, Jessica's parents and finally Jess, then left the church.

"We learned about Abraham and Sarah having an old baby," Nathan said.

"An old baby?" Brother Henry asked, grinning.

Nathan laughed and corrected, "Having a baby when they were old, I meant." He held out his palm and cocked his head at the preacher. "I remembered what I learned."

Brother Henry laughed. "I thought our deal was for you to remember *my* lessons."

"I didn't get to hear you preaching tonight," Nathan explained, and to his joy, Brother Henry dropped a peppermint in his hand.

"You're right. You didn't, and I'm glad you remembered what you learned in class. You're a smart boy, Nathan Bowman."

"That's what Mama says," Nathan said, working his words around the candy he'd already popped in his mouth.

Still laughing at Nathan's comments, Jessica and her parents steered him out of the church and to the car, where he talked about Abraham and Sarah the whole way home. By the time they reached the house, they had heard his entire interpretation of Abraham "getting a promise, and Sarah not believing it, and Sarah laughing, and then how they named him Isaac 'cause God said to 'cause she laughed and Isaac means laugh."

Nathan had enjoyed the story so much that he continued to talk about it throughout his bath and was still going strong when Jessica tucked him into bed.

"She laughed," Nathan said again, snuggling under the covers. "She didn't think God meant it, did she? That she would have a little boy when she was very old."

"Not at first," Jessica said. "But then later she did, especially when she had that little boy and she was so happy to have him, just like I'm happy to have you." She kissed his cheek and hugged him tightly, enjoying the bonding time they shared each night before he went to sleep.

Then she saw his rolled-up take-home papers on his nightstand and remembered what Hannah had said. "Hey, you didn't show me what you did in class. Want to show me before you go to sleep?"

"Sure," Nathan said, wriggling away from her to reach for the papers.

"This is Abraham and Sarah and Isaac," he said, pointing to the coloring page. "I kind of got out of the lines on her hair, but Ms. Hannah said I still did pretty good."

"She's right. You did a good job," Jess agreed. She continued admiring the picture and wondered why Hannah thought this paper showed that Nathan wants to meet his daddy. Maybe he'd said something about Abraham and the way he was looking at the baby in Sarah's arms. "So, you like this picture of Abraham's family?" Jess prompted, hoping to figure out what Hannah had meant.

"Yep, but my family is on the other side. We drew ours on the back." He turned the page, and Jessica now knew that this was what Hannah wanted her to see.

Nathan drew his typical tall, skinny house in red crayon and put an even taller tree on the right side, the green swirled circles at the top forming its leaves. On the ground, to the left of the house were two stick people. The taller one had brown hair that was longer, and Jess recognized the "mommy" drawing that Nathan often put in his pictures. She also recognized the little boy beside the mommy as his traditional "Nathan" drawing. Both of the stick people were merely round circle heads with two lines forming the legs, which was the extent of Nathan's current drawing skills.

Jessica adored the way he always drew the mommy and little boy so close together when he depicted his family. But the mommy and son weren't the only things on the page this time. On the opposite side of the house, just beneath the tree, was another stick figure, a little taller than the mommy, who appeared to be wearing a hat. And beside that circular head and string legs was another straight line extending outward, as though the fellow had one arm.

"Who's that?" Jess asked, though she suspected she knew.

"That's my daddy. He hasn't found us yet."

Jess nodded, gathering her bearings. *He doesn't even know to look for you yet.* "What's that?" she asked, pointing to that extended line.

"That's his bat," Nathan said, as though this should have been obvious. "Remember? He's going to teach me to play T-ball. And he's going to be my coach. Anson's daddy is his T-ball coach."

"Who's Anson?"

"A boy at school."

"Is that what he's wearing? His baseball cap?" She pointed to the hat on the daddy's head.

"Yep. Anson said he was on the Rangers last year, but he don't know what team he'll get this year yet. Do you think I'll get on Rangers or something else?"

"I don't know," Jess said, and made a mental note to check into the Claremont Little League sign-ups tomorrow. And she guessed she should probably ask how they go about signing up to coach.

She almost laughed, picturing her telling Chad that he had a son and then asking him to sign up for coaching duty. It was nearly funny, if it would only be that easy.

"Are you thinking that Daddy will find us soon?" she asked, trying to use Nathan's own terminology to describe what was bound to happen in the next few days.

"Yep."

"Me, too," she whispered, and Nathan smiled broadly. "When?"

"I'm thinking he'll find you in the next few days," she said. Then she thought about the other part of this equation, the one Nathan didn't know about yet. "And Nathan, do you remember when you told me you'd like a little brother or sister?"

"Yes!" he said, letting go of the paper in his excitement at the possibility. The sheet flittered off the bed to land on the floor.

Jess decided to wait about picking it up. This was more important. She cupped her palms beneath Nathan's face and looked into those excited green-gold eyes. "Well, when your daddy finds us, he may bring you a little sister with him."

"Really?" he asked. "Cool!" He moved his head away from her hands and peered past her to the floor. "Mama, get that for me," he said, then thought about what was missing in that request and added, "Please." He pointed to the paper on the floor. "And I need a color." He paused, grinned. "Please."

Jessica handed him the paper and then withdrew a box of crayons from his nightstand drawer. "You want a crayon?"

"Yeah, a red one." The paper had already started curling back up on the ends, and he worked to flatten it back out. Jessica grabbed the David and Goliath book that was still on the nightstand from when her father read him the story and placed it in Nathan's lap. Then she put the paper on top of the hard surface so it'd be easier for him to color...whatever he planned to color.

"What are you doing?" she asked.

"You'll see." He continued trying to make the sides of the page lay down, but they continued curling up.

Jessica flattened her palms on the page and pushed them to the edges so she could hold the paper in place for her son.

"Thanks," Nathan said, placing the crayon next to the daddy figure on the paper. Then he shook his head, mumbled, "Nope" and moved the crayon to the other side, beside his Nathan figure. When he was done, there was a new, smaller figure added to the scene. A small, circular head and two string legs formed a child to Nathan's left. Mommy on the right, little girl on the left. And Daddy still on the far side.

Jessica didn't like the feeling she got from that.

"Why did you put her there?" she asked. "By you?"

"Because," Nathan said, "I'll have to teach her stuff."

She smiled. "Yes, you will."

He picked up the crayon box and frowned.

"What's wrong?"

"I don't know what color of hair she has."

"Yellow," Jess said. "I believe she has yellow."

He nodded, grabbed a yellow crayon and put a puff of yellow hair on top of the little girl.

"Very nice," she said.

"Now," Nathan said, when he'd determined the piece was done. "It's just like Ms. Hannah said." He handed her the yellow crayon, and Jess slid it back into the box, then put the crayons away.

"Like Ms. Hannah said?" she asked.

"This side is Abraham's family," he explained, turning the page for her to see the preprinted paper that he'd colored in class. He turned the page again and smiled. "And this one is mine."

Jessica blinked a few times to keep the tears at bay. The image was nice, except for the daddy being on the other side of the page. Maybe soon Nathan would see them all together.

Please, God, let it be that way. Nathan wants a real family.

And so do I.

Chapter Seven

The last thing Jessica had planned to do on Thursday afternoon was cancel her coffee plans with Chad, but nevertheless that's exactly what she was about to do, thanks to a bizarre telephone call from Nathan's teacher.

She dialed Chad's number as she crossed the quad toward the English building, and her English Comp class. He didn't answer, and she really didn't expect him to, since he was probably preparing to teach his last class for the day, but she didn't want to break their plans via text message.

She prayed he'd understand.

After his voice mail greeting ended, she waited for the tone and then spoke as clearly as she could, given how worried she was about her son—about *their* son. "Hey, I'm sorry. I can't do coffee tonight. Nathan's teacher called, and she thinks there might be something wrong with him," she said and then swallowed. She had to tell him more than that. "Not physically," she clarified, "socially." She shook her head, thinking about how awkward this was to say into a cell phone. She needed to actually talk to him about what Nathan's teacher said. She needed parental advice. "She asked me not to speak to him until she has a chance to try to figure out what's wrong. I guess she just wanted my permission to talk to him, and I told her she had it, that I'd wait about asking him anything, but now—now I'm thinking maybe I should talk to him tonight. I'm his mama, so I should probably be the one—"

The phone beeped and an automated voice informed her that she had exceeded the allotted time to leave a message. She was then informed that she could rerecord or delete her message. Jessica debated an attempt to try leaving the message again so she didn't sound so much like a paranoid mother, but it was time for her class to start, and she didn't have the willpower to try and start over. Yeah, she'd botched the message, and yes, she forgot to tell him she'd still like to go out with him tomorrow night. But she knew he would return her call, and maybe she didn't sound as pathetic as she thought.

She entered her class in the nick of time, rather than her usual early arrival, dropped into her customary front row seat and concentrated on staying focused throughout the class. Unfortunately, her attempt at concentration failed. The class ended, and she had no clue about what Ms. Smelding discussed. She should have just gone on home after her first class so she could've gotten to Nathan quicker. Jessica sighed dismally and began gathering her books.

"Here, honey." An elderly voice broke through her thoughts, and she looked up to see Ms. Smelding standing in front of her, a batch of stapled papers extended toward Jess.

Jessica glanced around and realized the rest of the class had already left while she was thinking about Nathan and gathering her things. "What's that?"

"My notes from today's lecture. Normally you don't miss a word I say. Today, I'd wager you didn't catch one. Never even saw you pick up your pen. So I figure I'll give you a freebie this week, since you're probably the only one in here who's actually trying to learn something." She pushed the papers toward Jessica's nose. "Better grab them quick. My niceness can only last so long, you know. It runs out with age."

Jessica took the papers. "Thank you. I'm sorry about being so distracted. My son's teacher called me after my first class and said she wanted my permission to talk to him tomorrow and that she suspects he may have a problem, socially." She shrugged and was a little embarrassed when her mouth quivered.

The older woman stepped closer, wrapped an arm around her shoulders. "Well, now, that explains everything. Nothing can tear at your heart more than thinking there's something wrong with one of your kids. I've got four of them, all boys, you know. Stair steps, that's what they were. Only six years' difference from the oldest to the youngest." She gave Jess a squeeze, then removed her arm and laughed. "They were a handful, let me tell you, but they turned out all right. Each of them had their quirks." She shrugged. "I suppose everyone does. Some things are real problems. Other things, not so much. Until you know something for sure, though, there's no sense worrying too much about it, in my opinion. My youngest, Tyler, was nearly two years old before he uttered a word. I took him to one doctor after another thinking something was wrong with the boy."

Jessica listened with interest. "And was there?"

Her teacher shook her head and laughed again. "Turned out that he never had to talk because all of his older brothers were always more than anxious to tell everybody what he wanted to say. As soon as they got out of the house and in school, Tyler chatted up a storm. In fact, I've often joked that it took us two years to teach him to talk and the rest of his life to teach him when to shut up."

Jessica grinned, feeling a little better. "Thanks for sharing that."

"He's an attorney now and sure enough talks his share, let me tell you. But I do remember how worried I was back then when I thought something was wrong with my baby. It's hard to think that your child is anything less than perfect. But in Tyler's case, he's fine. And now I've got a baker's dozen of grandchildren to boot, each of them with their share of problems, their share of differences." She moved to her desk and gathered her teaching materials. "I won't lie to you and tell you some concerns for my kids weren't warranted. But you'll make it through. You pray for him, don't you? Your little boy?"

"All the time."

"Best thing you can do. And just so you know, I've had my share of parent-teacher meetings, too, and have been on both sides of the table—the parent worried about my child and the teacher worried about a student. If his teacher wants to talk to him and asked your permission before doing so, it sounds like she has both of your best interests at heart."

"It seems so," Jessica agreed.

Strong, sturdy footsteps echoed as someone moved through the hall. They grew louder and faster until the owner of those long, steady strides stepped inside the classroom.

Chad Martin's presence seemed to overpower the room, and Jessica saw him in an entirely new light. Not as the best looking instructor on campus. Not as the boy she'd grown to love in high school. Or as the man she still cared about more than any other.

She saw Nathan's daddy.

"I just got your message. What's happening with Nathan? What did his teacher say, exactly? I understand that you want to go home and see him soon, but I thought you might want to talk about it first."

Ms. Smelding tucked her teaching materials against her chest. "Hello, Mr. Martin," she said. Then to Jessica she said, "You two are welcome to talk in my classroom, if you like. I'm headed home, and there aren't any other classes in here tonight." She turned back to Chad. "Lock the door when you leave?"

"Yes, thank you, Ms. Smelding."

"You're welcome, son." She moved past Chad toward the door. "I'll say a prayer for your boy."

Jessica's breath caught in her throat. For a moment, it appeared Ms. Smelding was talking to Chad, but then she realized that her words were addressed to Jess.

"Thank you," she said and watched the older woman leave.

Chad wasted no time crossing the room, taking her books from her tight grasp and putting them back on her desk. "Come here, let me help." He pulled her against him, his strong arms wrapping around her and folding her into his warmth. "It'll be okay," he soothed.

The compassion in his voice, the sincerity of his embrace and concern for what she was going through pushed Jessica over the edge, and she finally released her tears.

"It's okay," he repeated softly, brushing his hand down her hair and holding her close. "I'll help you. Let me help you, Jess. I know you're worried about him, but you're not on your own here."

He didn't say another thing, allowing her to let go of the emotions that she'd held in check throughout the afternoon, ever since she received that call. She pressed her face against his shirt and felt the sturdy, solid beat of his heart against her cheek. Her tears trickled freely, and she let them fall. The weight of her worry lessened as each drop released, as though transferring through her tears from herself to the strong, compelling man that held her close.

Eventually, her tears subsided, and she sniffed, then eased away from his chest to look into those green-gold eyes. Chad's eyes. Nathan's eyes.

He gently, tenderly brushed her tears away. "You ready to talk about it?"

He was wearing jeans and a pale blue dress shirt with a big damp spot on the chest, right beside the green Polo Ralph Lauren logo. Apparently she'd lost more than tears, since the black residue on that spot looked like a good portion of the mascara she'd been wearing had also marred his nice shirt. She assumed the rest of it was smeared across her face.

Chad looked down, saw the spot that held her attention. One corner of his mouth lifted. "I was taking it to the cleaners anyway."

"I must be a mess," she whispered, attempting a ladylike dab beneath each eye and then viewing even more black smeared across her fingers. "I didn't realize I put on that much mascara."

He laughed, low and easy, reached for the tissue box at the corner of Ms. Smelding's desk and extracted a tissue, then a few more for good measure. "Here."

"Thanks." She made an effort to do a better job cleaning her face, then looked at him. "How'd I do?"

She could tell by the tightness of his jaw that he was working hard to keep from laughing at her attempt. He took one of the tissues from her hand and lightly rubbed the top of each cheek. She wouldn't have thought the black would have traveled that far.

"That's better," he said, tilting his head from one side to the other as he surveyed his handiwork. "So, are you ready to talk about it? You said Nathan's teacher thinks he has a problem socially?"

Jessica inhaled, nodded, then let it out.

"Did she say what she meant, exactly?" he asked, edging his hip on the desk then indicating the spot beside him for her to sit down, too.

Jess sat on the desk and was comforted again when he draped a supportive arm around her as she spoke. "She said that she noticed Nathan was a little distant last week when the kids would go to the gym to play. She said all of the boys would typically gather together to play basketball or jump rope together or something else that involved, you know, a group effort. But Nathan remained by himself."

"Last week was his first week at the new school, though, right? You'd mentioned you were worried about moving him in the middle of the year, and it makes sense that a kid would take a little time adjusting to a new school, new home, new friends. Did she mention that or take that into consideration?"

Jessica nodded. "She did, and I brought that up as well, which is why she said she didn't call me last week. She wanted to give him a little time to adjust to his new surroundings."

"Okay, so what happened to make her call this week?" he asked.

"This week, since we've had prettier weather and all, they've moved outside to the playground behind the school. It's full of things that encourage the kids to play together. Lots of playground equipment, a tall monkey bars set, seesaws, sandboxes, swing sets, kickball courts, tether ball, four-square corners, you name it."

"Sounds like they've added a lot since we went to Claremont Elementary. I remember playing kickball and four-square and the one big swing set, but that's it," he said, and she nodded.

"They've got everything now." She recalled taking Nathan to look at the school before he actually started. "That was his favorite thing about his new school, that the playground was so much larger than the one at his old school. He was even talking about all of the things he could do on that playground. I envisioned him playing nonstop, making lots of new friends." She paused, swallowed. "Everything that *normal* five-year-olds do on a playground." She stopped. Everything that normal five-year-olds do. Nathan's teacher thought he had a problem. She'd insinuated that perhaps Nathan wasn't "normal."

"But that's not what happened this week, when they

went outside?" Chad said, and she could tell that he was trying to bring her back to the conversation and away from the thoughts that were apparently showing her concern on her face.

"No," Jess said. "Nathan went to one of the sandboxes each day and played on his own. The boys in the class gathered on the play equipment the first day, but he stayed in the sandbox. Mrs. Carter, his teacher, still assumed he was trying to adjust, so she thought she'd coordinate a group activity the next day to help him fit in and to kind of force the other boys to include him, I suppose."

"What kind of activity?"

"She got out there with them and organized a kickball game. Her teacher's aide had the girls, and she had the boys." Jessica paused, thinking about the playground filled with children, boys and girls all laughing and playing together…and Nathan off to the side. Alone.

"And Nathan? He didn't join in?"

She shook her head. "She said he stayed at the sandbox, and when she urged him to join in, he told her he was busy, that he was building a bridge and needed to finish it."

Chad's eyes changed, brightening a bit with her comment, and then to Jessica's shock, the corners of his mouth lifted in a brilliant smile. "He told her he needed to finish his bridge."

Jess didn't really understand why this was funny. "Yes."

"And he didn't want to be bothered with playing because he had a bridge to build," Chad said, now laughing amid his words.

Jessica blinked, tried to understand what part of

Nathan's actions made Chad think that this wasn't serious. Her child was isolating himself from other children his age. That wasn't normal; his teacher had said so, and Jess believed her. And now that she'd confided in Chad, in Nathan's father, he was making light of the problem. A prickle of frustration worked its way through her senses, and she wanted to tell him that he was laughing at Nathan. That he was making fun of their son.

But she couldn't. She didn't dare.

She opened her mouth to tell him she didn't appreciate his behavior, but before she could say a word, Chad held up a hand.

"I'm sorry, Jess. It's just that I've never heard of another child behaving that way before, and now I realize how my mother must have felt back then."

"Your mother?"

"When my first grade teacher called her in for the same thing." He smiled. "I mean, it sounds so similar to what she was told, and your Nathan is acting the same way, well, that I did when I was about his age." He laughed. "Sounds like your little guy has one of my quirks."

"One of your quirks?" she asked and didn't dare say anything else. All it would take was an affirmation that Nathan would naturally have inherited some of Chad's traits and Chad would know the truth. But telling him now, here, in Ms. Smelding's classroom, didn't feel right. Plus, she still didn't know what quirk Chad was referring to. Thankfully, he explained.

"When I was in first grade, my teacher called Mom in for a parent-teacher conference. That was the year Dad ran out on us, so naturally, when Mrs. O'Ryan explained that I was isolating myself from the remainder of the class, she and my mother determined that I was unable to cope with the loss of my father and that I was losing the ability to connect with anyone socially. She recommended Mom take me to a child psychiatrist for evaluation."

"You went to a child psychiatrist? As a first grader?"

"Still remember it," Chad said, and his mouth quirked to the side as he apparently recalled the visit to the doctor's office. "They called it play therapy, where basically she took me into a room filled with toys, got on the floor beside me and we played."

"Do you think Nathan needs to go to a psychiatrist?" she asked, unable to disguise in her voice the dread that image portrayed.

"No, I don't. Because I'm betting you'd be wasting a bunch of money, just like my mother wasted a bunch back then, when my problem wasn't really a problem with my societal skills." Chad grinned and pronounced, "If he's got the same 'issues' I had, and it sure sounds like he does, then all that a psychiatrist would tell you is that your little boy is advanced for his age."

"Advanced?" Jessica's heart fluttered at the possibility. Then again, Chad had always been at the top of his class in school, for as long as she could remember. He'd been valedictorian of his class and had only taken three years to obtain his premed degree. And while Jessica's academic accomplishments weren't *that* superb, she had always done well in school and actually had a chance at the top of her class, if she hadn't left to have Nathan. Even doing that, though, she'd obtained her high school diploma through summer night classes in Tennessee. And she'd always done well—very well—with her grades.

Wouldn't it make sense that Nathan would be advanced for his age? Odd that she'd never considered it before. But he was a smart boy, a very smart boy, and he did love to learn.

"You're considering it, aren't you, that you're raising a boy genius." The way Chad said it, and the way he was obviously putting himself in the former boy genius category, made Jessica's smile easy.

"Okay," she said. "I can see that he could potentially be advanced for his age, but how does this whole sandbox thing play into that? Obviously, you're the expert on it." Her voice was teasing, playful. Now that she believed Nathan was probably okay, and moreover, that he was so like his daddy that way, she actually felt a little giddy. Happy. Excited.

"I didn't claim to be an expert, but I did see a psychiatrist for basically the same thing," he said, smiling.

Jess really liked his smile. "So, tell me. What did they say about you?"

"During our play therapy, that psychiatrist had me building things with her. I remember she had this electric K'NEX set, a big crane, in the center of the floor. I was drawn to it, mesmerized by it. I couldn't wait to figure out how it worked, to control it and to do something that was obviously so much beyond what I 'should' be doing at my age. She'd been surprised when I picked that toy, which I now know was meant for kids eight and up."

Jessica nodded and thought about all of the trips to Toys "R" Us when Nathan begged her for some type of building toy where the recommended age on the outside of the box was well beyond his five years. She'd always managed to lure him away from the object of his desire and thought at the time that she was helping him, keeping him from being frustrated later when the toy was beyond his ability. She silently resolved to change her tactic next time. They could try the more difficult toy together, or if he'd rather, she could give him time to solve the puzzle of the model on his own. Maybe that would build his confidence, increase his self-esteem when he accomplished something so difficult.

"In the process of watching me learn the details of how to put the crane together and eventually how to run the motorized sculpture, the psychiatrist asked me a simple question about what I liked best about playing with the other kids at school."

"And you said…"

He laughed, apparently recalling the discussion. "I told her that they weren't nearly as much fun as playing with that crane. They played easy games. I liked the hard ones."

Jessica smirked. Chad had always liked a challenge and apparently Nathan did, too. But still, she wasn't sure how that played into her son—their son—abandoning his classmates on the playground in exchange for solitude in the sandbox. "But Nathan isn't playing harder games," she said. "Mrs. Carter said he's playing in the sandbox."

"What did she say he was doing last week, when they couldn't go outside and were confined to playing in the gym?" Chad had such an assuredness about his tone that Jessica already suspected he had an answer to her problem. And consequently, she already felt better about the situation.

"She said that he spent his time with the obstacle course materials."

Chad's brows knitted, as though this explanation didn't follow through with what he'd expected. "Running an obstacle course by himself?"

"No," Jess said. "He took the materials for the course—the cones, barrels, plastic crates," she started, and Chad held up a hand to stop her.

Grinning broadly, he proclaimed, "And he built something."

Jess nodded and again felt instantly better that Chad seemed to have an answer for Nathan's behavior. "Mrs. Carter thought he was working on a rocket, from what she determined, but she said she would ask him more about it tomorrow, when they talked."

Chad's smile continued. "He needed more of a challenge than the other activities going on around him, so he made one up." He lifted one shoulder and lifted a hand, insinuating the problem was now solved. "Your boy is like me, and I turned out okay, didn't I?"

Jessica felt her throat tighten, her heart rate increase on its own accord. She should tell him, right here, right now.

"Chad," she started, but he interrupted her.

"I know, I know, I should have been a doctor," he joked. And then he paused, and his smile faded.

"You'd have been a great doctor," she said and felt the weight of the conversation shift, where she was now the comforter, Chad the one needing comfort. He'd wanted that so much in high school, and she still wondered what brought him here, to Stockville Community College, to teach. "And you got your premed degree early. That obviously says that your boy genius status has simply become man genius status now." She frowned. "That doesn't sound quite right."

He laughed, and the sadness she'd seen in his eyes a moment ago dissipated. "That's okay. You can call me man genius anytime you want. I'll learn to live with it."

That caused her to laugh, too.

"One more thing though, about Nathan."

She swallowed. She should have told him because this conversation must have given away too much. But she so thought this wasn't the right time and that tomorrow, when they shared their first real date, would be the perfect time to tell him about their son. "What about Nathan?" she forced herself to ask.

"He does play with other kids sometimes, doesn't he? I mean, he enjoys being around kids his age, but he just gets bored with them at times." Apparently, Chad recognized that a complete lack of social skills wouldn't be a good thing, no matter whether her child was a "boy genius" like his father, or not.

Jessica found an easy answer for this question, and it hadn't been long since she'd seen affirmation of the fact. "He does like playing with other kids, but usually the activity has to be something that's a bit of a test. Like Wednesday night, at the end of his church class, he and several of the other kids worked together to put a Noah's ark puzzle together." She remembered the children all gathered together and finding their way through the cut pieces to form the animal-filled boat.

Chad nodded, satisfied. "Wait and see what the teacher says tomorrow, after she's talked to him, but I'm betting you're about to get news similar to what my mother got way back then. He's simply wanting to do harder activities, and when his buddies are conducting one, he makes up his own. It's okay. And in the long run, it'll help you out."

"How's that?"

"He'll be the type of kid who can always entertain himself. I know I was. In fact, I'd wager my experiments entertained Becky, too."

His experiments. Jess recalled something Becky had told her about when they were in middle school. "Didn't you blow up your kitchen?"

He chuckled. "Becky exaggerates. Blowing it up is a bit strong of a term." He paused for effect. "Let's just say after I practiced with my sixth grade science experiment, a real working volcano, Mom had a good reason for renovating the kitchen."

She laughed. "Great. So now I know I have plenty to look forward to while Nathan is entertaining himself."

"Pretty much," Chad agreed, easing off the desk. "So, you feel better now?"

"Much," she admitted. "Thanks."

He checked his watch. They'd been talking over an hour. "We can still go get that coffee if you want, but I'm betting you're probably ready to go home and hug him before he goes to bed." He picked up her books. "Right?"

"Yes," she said, also sliding off the desk. "But we can add coffee to the end of our night tomorrow if that works into your plans."

"I think that could be arranged." He walked beside her toward the door, locked the classroom and then continued with her down the now empty hall.

A few late classes were still in session, judging from the low rumble of teacher's voices echoing off the tiled walls. Still, their walk through the building and then out across the quad to the parking area seemed private, intimate. Jessica sensed a connection between them now, as though they walked as one, thought as one. And she thought she knew why.

Chad had helped her through her first difficult issue with Nathan. He'd been there, right beside her, to analyze the situation and then determine what was happening to their son, and why. It was the first time she'd had anyone truly help her with her parenting skills, and Chad was the only person she'd have wanted filling that void.

She'd needed him.

They approached her car. As they crossed the quad, she'd withdrawn her keys from her pocket. She didn't even recall the act, but Chad had noticed and took them to unlock the door. Then he opened it and waited for her to slide inside. He then reached across her and placed her books on the passenger seat, and Jessica inhaled the spicy, masculine scent of his cologne.

"Chad," she whispered.

"Yes," he said, reaching across her once more to fasten her seatbelt in place.

"Thank you for everything."

He paused, his face mere inches from her as he leaned into the car. "I meant it, Jess, when I told you that I want a relationship with you. And having one with you means having one with Nathan." He grinned. "And it means you having one with Lainey, which you've already started. She adored you, you know."

"She's a precious little girl."

"Well, you're ahead of me there. I've still yet to meet your little guy. But I'm looking forward to it, especially now that I know he and I have something in common, geniuses and all."

HOW TO VALIDATE YOUR EDITOR'S FREE GIFTS! "THANK YOU"

1. Peel off the FREE GIFTS SEAL from front cover. Place it in the space provided at right. This automatically entitles you to receive two free books and two exciting surprise gifts.
2. Send back this card and you'll get 2 Love Inspired® books. These books have a combined cover price of $11.00 for the regular-print and $12.50 for the larger-print in the U.S. and $13.00 for the regular-print or $14.50 for the larger-print in Canada, but they are yours to keep absolutely FREE!
3. There's no catch. You're under no obligation to buy anything. We charge nothing—ZERO—for your first shipment. And you don't have to make any minimum number of purchases—not even one!
4. We call this line Love Inspired because every month you'll receive books that are filled with joy, faith and traditional values. The stories will lift your spirit and warm your heart! You'll like the convenience of getting them delivered to your home well before they are in stores. And you'll love our discount prices, too!
5. We hope that after receiving your free books you'll want to remain a subscriber. But the choice is yours—to continue or cancel, anytime at all! So why not take us up on our invitation, with no risk of any kind. You'll be glad you did!
6. And remember...just for validating your Editor's Free Gifts Offer, we'll send you 2 books and 2 gifts, *ABSOLUTELY FREE!*

YOURS FREE!

We'll send you two fabulous surprise gifts (worth about $10) absolutely FREE, simply for accepting our no-risk offer!

The Reader Service —Here's How It Works:

Accepting your 2 free books and 2 free gifts (gifts valued at approximately $10.00) places you under no obligation to buy anything. You may keep the books and gifts and return the shipping statement marked "cancel." If you do not cancel, about a month later we will send you 6 additional books and bill you just $4.24 each for the regular-print edition or $4.74 each for the larger-print edition in the U.S. or $4.74 each for the regular-print edition or $5.24 each for the larger-print edition in Canada. That is a savings of at least 23% off the cover price. It's quite a bargain! Shipping and handling is just 50¢ per book in the U.S. and 75¢ per book in Canada.* You may cancel at any time, but if you choose to continue, every month we'll send you 6 more books, which you may either purchase at the discount price or return to us and cancel your subscription.

*Terms and prices subject to change without notice. Prices do not include applicable taxes. Sales tax applicable in N.Y. Canadian residents will be charged applicable taxes. Offer not valid in Quebec. All orders subject to credit approval. Credit or debit balances in a customer's account(s) may be offset by any other outstanding balance owed by or to the customer. Please allow 4 to 6 weeks for delivery. Offer available while quantities last.

Jessica was overwhelmed by the realization that Nathan would meet his father before the week ended, and, like Nathan had said last Sunday in the car, he was "gonna love him."

Chapter Eight

Chad's mother was only forty-seven, but her hair had been solid white for as long as he could remember. In Chad's mind, her premature gray occurred approximately the same year that his father had left them. However, though she'd often been exhausted and definitely stressed at trying to make ends meet on her own with two children, Mae Martin never complained. And she never let her children believe that there wasn't anything they couldn't accomplish.

She entered Chad's house with her tan overnight bag draped across her shoulder and a red teddy bear in her hand. "Hey, sorry I'm late. They were putting out the Valentine's display at work, and I wanted to get Lainey something." She indicated the bear. "Isn't it precious?"

The bear held a white heart with Too Cute embroidered across the center.

"Very precious, just like our little lady," Chad said, holding the little lady and kissing her cheek. "Look what Grandma brought you, Lainey."

Lainey's smile stretched into her cheeks, and she

reached out, not so much for the bear, but for her grandma. "Gamma."

Chad's mother dropped her overnight case on the couch and took Lainey. "How's my little angel?"

"She's great," Chad said. "And she's been pretty excited all afternoon. I told her you were coming to spend the night."

Lainey accepted her teddy bear and snuggled her nose against his face. "Tank oo."

"You're welcome, darling," his mother said. "I'm glad you asked me to stay here tonight. Lainey does seem to do better when she sleeps in her own bed, and I didn't want you rushing to get home early to pick her up from my place. This way, if you and Jessica want to go to a late movie, you don't have to worry."

"I appreciate that, Mom."

"No, I appreciate the chance to spend time with her."

"I've got her dinner ready and was just about to put her in the high chair," he said.

"I could've done that," his mother said, frowning a bit.

"I know, but you've worked all day, and I didn't want you to have to worry about cooking, either. I fixed enough for you, too. Nothing special, chicken fingers and mashed potatoes."

"Lainey's favorite," his mom said, following him into the kitchen and locating one of Lainey's oversize dinner bibs on the counter. She snapped the pink bib in place and then put Lainey in her chair.

Lainey clapped when she saw her plate, then scooped up her sippy cup and started working on her juice.

"Okay, you'll probably need to head out, right?" his mother said. "Don't worry about us. We'll be fine."

"I know," Chad said, kissing the top of Lainey's head and inhaling the sweet scent of her baby shampoo. "Love you, sweetie."

Lainey's lips smacked as she released the sippy cup. "Wuv oo."

"I didn't mention it before, but I wanted to let you know that I'll probably need to leave early in the morning. That's okay, right?" she said, turning away from him and busying herself with the dishwasher.

Chad knew why she hadn't mentioned it, and he also knew why she was avoiding looking at him. "You're working tomorrow? I thought you weren't working Saturdays anymore. Is there something you need, Mom, because I can give you—"

She audibly exhaled, turned back to him and smiled. "Honey, I don't need you to give me anything else. You do way too much for me as it is."

"I'd like to do more," he said, as he often did. She let him buy her a decent car and she'd accepted the fact that he was determined to put a nice sum of spending money in her bank account each month, but she wouldn't let him support her completely, no matter how many times he asked. Chad was making good money now, and she'd struggled her entire life, working until she could barely stand up, all because she never wanted Chad or Becky to want for anything. He simply wanted her to be able to rest and enjoy life for a change. "And if you don't need me to help, why are you going in on a Saturday?"

"I volunteered. They're shorthanded at the store tomorrow, just for the early hours. I'll be done by eight, and I thought I'd come back here then so you can go to your practice."

"My practice?"

She pointed to the calendar on the side of the refrigerator where Chad had notated that tomorrow morning was the first baseball practice for the local men's league. He'd signed up last year and found that he really enjoyed getting out and burning off some energy with other guys his age. Most teams didn't start practicing until February, since the first game wasn't until mid-March but Chad and his friends were anxious to get started. And they really liked to win. Plus, his mom enjoyed keeping Lainey while he went, and once it started warming up, she'd even brought her to the games. "You don't need to miss the first one." She closed the dishwasher and moved to the table to sit beside Lainey while she gnawed on a piece of chicken.

"It wouldn't have been a problem for Jess and I to change our plans to tomorrow night," he said.

"No, indeed. This isn't just some ordinary date. This is Jessica Bowman." She paused, helped Lainey guide a spoonful of potatoes to her mouth. "I never knew what happened back then between you two, but I know that you still loved her long after she moved away. And I know that she was a good girl, an honest girl. *She* wouldn't have lied to you."

Chad knew what she was thinking. Jessica wouldn't have lied to him—not like Kate. But his mother wouldn't complete the sentence, not with Lainey nearby. Even though she was only eighteen months old, they were very protective of everything she heard that concerned her mother. And unfortunately, there wasn't anything good that could be said for Kate, except that she'd given him

Lainey. For that, he'd always be grateful to her, in spite of the pain she'd put him through.

"I'm telling Jessica tonight," he said.

The spoon stopped momentarily as his mother processed that. "About Kate?" she asked, her mouth flattening as she guided the potatoes to her granddaughter's waiting open mouth.

Lainey swallowed, reached for her juice and slurped. Then she turned her attention back to the chicken, which she could handle easily on her own. Chad's mother took the opportunity to focus on her son.

"What, exactly, are you telling her?" she asked.

"Everything."

She nodded, as though she'd known and expected, no less. "About Lainey, too, then."

"Yes."

She leaned toward her granddaughter, ran her lips across Lainey's baby soft curls. "Such a little darling. And to think, what could have happened."

Chad didn't want to think about it, but he'd have to tonight because he didn't want to start a relationship with Jessica unless she knew and understood everything about Kate. And Lainey. "Mom, you know how I feel about Jess. And if we're going to be together I don't want any secrets between us."

"I know."

"I want her to know about what happened during the years we were apart, and I'm wanting to learn the same about her. There's something I haven't told you about Jess. She has a son. His name is Nathan." He'd talked to his mother several times since he and Jessica had run into each other on the college campus, and he'd told her about her returning to school, working in the day care, spending time with Lainey.

However, he hadn't told her about Jessica's little boy. He hadn't wanted her opinion of Jess to change, and like she'd said earlier, she'd always seen Jessica Bowman as a good girl. Which was only right. Jess was a good girl, an honest girl. Yes, she'd had a baby before marriage, but he didn't want that marring his mother's opinion. Now he wanted to hear her say it didn't.

"She has a son?" Her green eyes widened a bit, mouth rolled inward as though she were trying to comprehend the reality.

"More," Lainey said. She'd dropped the spoon, since Grandma was handling it better anyway, and now waited to be fed. She opened her mouth wider, emphasizing her request.

Mae smiled at her and fed her another spoonful, then another, while Chad waited for more of a response. Finally, when Lainey grabbed her sippy again, she said, "His name is Nathan?"

"Yes, and he's actually in kindergarten at Claremont Elementary. She was a little nervous about moving him midyear, but he's doing okay." Chad grinned. "He likes spending time on his own, and Jess was a bit worried about that, but I reminded her how you and Mrs. O'Ryan had been concerned about me for the same reason, and I think he's going to be just fine."

She'd started breaking up additional bits of chicken for Lainey, and her hands paused for a moment. "He's in kindergarten?"

"Yes."

"Have you met him?" Her question came quick, as though she was concerned about the possibility of Chad meeting Jessica's son. But Chad wasn't concerned at all. He knew he'd get along with Nathan as well as she got along with Lainey. And after his conversations with her last night about Nathan, he now had a bit of insight to what the boy liked—primarily a challenge. In fact, he'd surfed the net awhile this afternoon looking at building sets for kids over eight. True, Nathan was five, but he liked a challenge, and Chad was definitely the right guy to help him out. That'd be a great way to bond, too, creating something together.

Chad couldn't wait—not only to play with the little boy but to grow closer to a child who was a part of Jessica.

"Have you? Met him yet?" his mother asked again, and she seemed to be trying to control the urgency of her tone.

"No," he said, grinning. "But if I don't meet him tonight when I pick her up, I'll definitely meet him tomorrow. We're taking Nathan and Lainey to Hydrangea Park to feed the ducks."

She inhaled, and Chad thought she was going to say more, but then she remained silent.

"I'm sure Nathan and I will hit it off," he assured.

Her smile was genuine now. And she nodded. "I'm sure you will." She blinked a few times, and Chad noticed her eyes glistening, the way they always did when her emotions were getting the best of her.

"Mom, it'll be okay."

"Do you know anything about Nathan's father?" she asked hesitantly.

"I know that Jessica loved him, and I know that he didn't want to marry her." He paused. "I'm hoping she'll open up and talk to me about it tonight. Nathan's a big part of her life, and I'm praying that means he'll be a big part of my life, too."

"He didn't want to marry her?" Her head cocked to the side, eyes squinted as though finding this completely absurd.

"I don't understand either, but she said he never asked. Like I said, I'm planning for us to talk, about both of our pasts, tonight. And then, I'd really like the two of us to stop talking about the past—and concentrate on the future."

"You always loved her."

It wasn't a question, and Chad didn't have to answer. She knew.

Lainey's head rested against her shoulder. Her hands were no longer making any effort to maneuver the food on her plate, and her eyes paused between blinks. Her grandmother noticed and eased her out of the chair.

"I think we'll take a bath and put on jammies." She looked at Chad. "Jessica is staying with her parents now?"

"Until she finds a place of her own."

"I haven't seen them in a while. Maybe I'll give them a call, you know, and catch up." She drew Lainey close. "I suppose I'd have seen them, maybe would have kept up with Jessica more if I'd have kept going to church."

Chad didn't know what to say to that. His mother hadn't been on the best of terms with God in a long time. She'd taken him and Becky to church when they were young and when they all went together as a family. When he still had a father at home. After his dad left so did her faith.

But a few times during his high school years, Chad had convinced her to come. Easter, Christmas and a couple of special services when the teens were putting on plays for the church and Jessica had encouraged him and Becky to take a part. Chad remembered standing on the stage dressed as a shepherd and seeing his mother sitting on a pew beside Jessica's folks and big, wet droplets falling like water down her cheeks. She'd never discouraged Chad or Becky to have a relationship with God; she just hadn't been able to muster one up herself.

But Chad suspected that deep down she wanted to go back. And he thought that perhaps God was showing him an opening to help her make that happen. "I want Lainey to grow up going to church," he said, and instantly recalled Jessica's similar statement. "We've been a few times, but it hasn't been consistent. And I think it's important and that it, well, that it'll make her life better, if she goes."

Her mouth quivered involuntarily before she seemed to regain control. "I think so, too," she whispered.

"But I honestly believe that it's important for the whole family to go, together," he added.

Again, she nodded. "I do, too, honey. And I would love for that to be the case for you and Jessica and Nathan and Lainey. Wouldn't that be something, after all these years, for you two, and your children, to be a real family? It'd be—" she paused "—a dream come true."

He suspected she wasn't only talking about his dreams. She was talking about hers. But she didn't understand Chad's statement.

"Mom," he said, moving closer to her and running a palm across the back of Lainey's head, now slumped on her shoulder as she slept.

"Yes?" she asked.

"When I say I want the whole family to go together,

I mean the whole family. I want you there, Mom. And more important than that, I'm certain that God wants you there, too."

A single tear slipped free. "I don't know. It's been a long time." She gave a watery smile. "I'm not sure He even remembers me."

"How could He forget the best mother in the world?" Chad asked, pronouncing her with the very words that he always used to describe Mae Martin, and meaning every syllable. He loved her with all of his heart, appreciated everything she'd done for him more than he could ever express, and he wanted her to have everything he could give her and more. And the thing that was most important and that he believed would help her find true happiness...was God.

She sniffed, patted Lainey's back. "Hey, you're going to be late, and this is an important night."

Chad moved closer, kissed her cheek. "I love you, Mom."

"I love you, too." She started across the kitchen toward the hall.

"You'll think about it? Church on Sunday? Because I'm planning to take Lainey, and Jessica will be there with Nathan, I'm sure. It's important that I meet him, but it's important for him to know you, too."

"I'll think about it," she promised, and Chad nodded. For now, that was all he could ask. That and one more thing.

God, be with me tonight. Give me the courage to tell Jessica about everything that happened with Kate. And help her to trust me enough to talk to me, really talk to me, about what happened to her over the past six years. Help us to nurture this bond we have and help it be even stronger than it was back then. He heard the water starting in the bathroom, listened as Lainey woke to the sound and started chatting about her bath. *And God, be with Mom. Help her to find You again, and help her to find happiness again. Let her see how a real family can be, with me.*

Chapter Nine

Jessica was glad that her work at the day care center kept her busy throughout the day. She could literally feel her anticipation for her date…and for the conversation that she would have with Chad tonight. Right now he knew he wanted a relationship with Jess and knew that he wanted to meet her son so they could introduce their children to the idea of the two of them together. In a few hours, he'd realize that the introduction was much more than that.

He would be introduced to his son.

"Jessica, are you okay?" Her mother stood at the doorway to the kitchen, her face showing unhidden concern. "Honey, it'll be all right. You've been planning to talk to him and tell him about Nathan for years. And it's the right thing. He should know that amazing little boy, and Nathan is going to adore his father."

"I know, Mom, but I also know how much it would have meant to Chad to be there for Nathan—and for me—the entire time. I don't know how he's going to handle the fact that I kept him from Nathan, even if I did what I believed was best at the time." Sitting on the couch, Jess fiddled with the belt on her dress. "Should I change?"

Her mother smiled. "You've changed twice already, and each outfit was fine. I like that dress. You've always looked good in red, and now is no different. Besides, Chad is going to think you're beautiful no matter what you're wearing." She moved to sit in the rocker facing the couch. "He was always in love with you, honey. And I can't imagine those feelings will be any less than they were back then, in spite of the years between. The two of you shared a special bond, and you share a son together, even if he doesn't know that yet."

"What if he can't forgive me?" The question had been at the heart of every thought Jess had throughout the day, and she couldn't shake it now.

Her mother eased out of the rocker, moved to the couch and scooted close to Jess. "Honey, you need to have faith in Chad and faith that God will help you through this time. Chad will forgive you."

"I don't know, Mom. I've kept him from his son for nearly six years. What if it simply isn't possible for him to forgive that?"

"I have a question for you. Who was it that said, 'With God, all things are possible?'"

Jessica swallowed. "Christ."

"Exactly. I tell you what, the best thing we can do right now is pray—pray that God will be with you tonight, right beside you when you have that tough conversation and pray that he will allow Chad to see the truth, that you did what you thought was best for him back then and that the best thing for both of you, and for your children, is to move forward."

Jessica nodded. "You're right."

Her mother took Jessica's hands in hers and prayed, "Dear Heavenly Father, be with Jess tonight. Help her to find strength in You as she tells Chad the truth. And be with Chad, that he opens his heart to the forgiveness she desires and to the love that she feels for him. Bless their relationship, Lord, and bless their children. In Christ's name, amen."

Footsteps sounded on the porch, and Jess quickly brushed away the tears that had pushed free during her mother's prayer.

"He's here," she whispered, as a solid rap knocked against the front door. "This is it. I've been waiting for this night since Nathan was born. And now it's here."

Her mother gave her hands a comforting squeeze and whispered, "Everything will be fine. Nothing's impossible with God on your side."

"You know what? You're right." Jessica smiled, aware that her nerves had eased with their prayer. In fact, she stood and walked to the door without any apprehension whatsoever. Oh, she was still anxious, but she was anxious to see the man on the other side of the door. Anxious to see the only guy she'd ever loved. Anxious to see the father of her son.

Another knock started as she turned the knob, and she pulled the door back to find Chad's fist balled and ready to pound again.

He laughed, dropped his arm and then snapped his mouth shut. Then he visibly took in Jessica's appearance, from her hair piled loosely on top of her head with long strands falling around her neck to the red dress, a wraparound jersey with crossover front that tied at her waist. "You look incredible."

Her mind flashed back to the first time he'd ever

picked her up at this house, when she was merely sixteen and they were headed to a school basketball game. He'd said the same thing, and her stomach had fluttered the same way it did now.

And just like that, any bit of nervousness that remained disappeared. Jessica was with her friend, and consequently with the man she loved, and she would let God help her figure out the tough spots as the night went on. For now, she wanted to enjoy the fact that tonight was literally a dream come true.

"Thanks," Jess said. Then, assuming turnabout was fair play, she took a small step back and eyed his appearance, too.

Chad, playing along, held out his arms and rotated for her review.

Stifling a giggle, Jessica took her time checking out his hair, the late afternoon sun drawing attention to the natural highlights. Then she noted how his deep green dress shirt matched the emerald in his eyes. And finally, the crisp khakis and dark leather shoes that tied everything together and made him look like he'd stepped off the cover of a magazine.

Or stepped right out of her dreams.

He tilted his head to the side and lifted a brow in an adorable *Well, do I pass inspection?* stance.

"You look amazing, too," she said, unwilling to even pretend that she wasn't impressed.

Obviously overhearing their banter, her mother chuckled lightly from her place on the couch, and Jessica pivoted to allow Chad inside. He grinned as he stepped through the doorway, then focused on her mom.

"Hello, Mrs. Bowman, how are you?" he asked, extending his hand as he neared the sofa.

She shook his hand and smiled at him affectionately. Jessica's parents had always loved Chad, and her mother's words were undeniably the truth when she said, "Wonderful to have you back at the house again, Chad."

He looked at Jessica. "Wonderful to be here again." He looked around the room. "Is your father home? And how about Nathan? I'm looking forward to meeting him."

Jessica had known Chad would ask when she recommended her father take Nathan to an afternoon movie. She did want him to meet Nathan, but she needed time to tell him everything first. Tonight, that would happen. She anticipated that, knowing Chad and that he would want to meet his son immediately after he learned the truth. So possibly, before this day ended, he would.

"Bryant took Nathan to the matinee," her mother explained when Jess didn't offer a quick response. "But I understand that all of you are going to Hydrangea Park tomorrow, right? So you'll get to see our precious boy soon."

"Yes, we're taking Lainey and Nathan to feed the ducks there tomorrow," Chad said. "It's supposed to be nice outside again, like today."

"I'm sure he'll have a fit over Lainey," Jessica's mother said. "She was so pretty all dressed up at church. And Nathan loves feeling like the big boy. I know he'll enjoy taking on that role when you go to the park. I'll make sure to have some bread ready for him to take to the ducks. And I'll have plenty enough for him to share with Lainey."

Chad quickly turned his attention back to Jessica, as though remembering something he'd forgotten. "I can't believe I forgot to ask. How did it go today with Nathan's teacher? Did she talk to him?"

"Yes, and I'm sorry, too. After you helped me so much with that last night, I forgot to let you know after she called. I had a lot on my mind," she said. Then she clarified, "I had our date on my mind."

"Same here," he agreed, grinning. "And I'm assuming since you're smiling, and since you're obviously still feeling like going out tonight, that you received good news from his teacher?"

"I did. It was almost exactly what you had predicted. It looks like I'm raising a boy genius." Her laugh matched the one her mother emitted from the couch.

"Sorry." Her mom stood from the sofa and held up her hands in a motion that asked forgiveness for her laughter. "It just seems a little strange to hear, even though I totally agree with everything Mrs. Carter said. Nathan wants a challenge, and from the sound of things, I believe she'll do her best to make sure he always has one."

"I'll tell you all about it in the car," Jessica said. "You said our reservation is at seven, right?"

Chad glanced at his watch. "Right, we better get going." He opened the door for Jessica. "Nice to see you, Mrs. Bowman."

"Very nice to see you, Chad," she said, and she gave Jessica her best don't-worry-everything-will-be-fine smile.

Jessica felt better merely seeing it. "Thanks, Mom. Give Nathan a kiss good night for me, okay?"

"You know I will."

Jessica walked with Chad to his car and waited for him to open her door.

"You're getting more used to it now, hmm?" he asked, winking as she slid into his car.

"I guess I am." A sense of first date giddiness flitted through her, and she giggled as he walked around the car to the driver's side.

The front door to the house opened, and her mother came out with a pink sheet of paper in her hand. "I nearly forgot to tell you about this," she said, approaching the car. "I wasn't sure what you were planning after dinner, but they've decorated the park already, and I thought you might enjoy it." She was a bit breathless from trying to catch them before they left, and she exhaled with a final "Whew" as she handed the pink flyer to Chad.

He took the paper and scanned the information on the page, printed beneath a sketch of the heart-shaped pond at Hydrangea Park. "I hadn't realized it was already time for the Valentine's display. I'd actually planned for us to go to a movie after dinner but this would beat a movie anytime. What do you think, Jess?"

The last time she'd been to see the Valentine lights display at the park had been over six years ago, and it'd been with Chad. "I think that'd be perfect."

They drove to the restaurant, and she told him all about her conversation with Mrs. Carter. He laughed when she quoted Nathan saying, "Sometimes those kids just get on my nerves, and I need some time with just me."

"That's hysterical. And even funnier because I know my mom heard something so similar when my teacher called her in."

Jessica laughed and silently wondered how many other things he and Nathan would have in common.

By the time they arrived at the restaurant, they'd

thoroughly covered her conversation with Mrs. Carter. Throughout dinner, they discussed Lainey, or more specifically, Chad's new phone, a purchase he'd been forced to make due to Lainey's infatuation with the previous one. She liked to pretend she was talking, and Chad let her. But then she'd been carrying it around one minute, and the next minute, it was gone. Chad had it on silent mode, so there was no hope of finding it by merely dialing the number and listening for the ring.

Jessica swallowed a bite of her lasagna, then asked, "So what did you do?"

He fished a shiny new iPhone out of his pocket. "Got it this morning. I can't be away from her without being accessible, and I promised myself that this one will stay out of tiny little hands, no matter how much she likes to push the buttons." He laughed, and Jessica did, too. He was obviously a terrific dad to Lainey, and he'd be a terrific dad to Nathan, too.

The waitress arrived with a plate filled with the dessert Messina's was famous for: fried strawberries.

"Oh, wow, I wish I hadn't eaten so much lasagna," Jessica said, eyeing the bright red pieces of fruit, assembled in a heart shape on the plate. Powdered sugar dotted the berries and a swirl of heart-shaped strawberry sauce centered the plate.

Chad picked up a berry, held it to his mouth and then bit into the fruit. He then made quite a display of humming his contentment while he chewed and then continuing to sound his pleasure as he swallowed. "That's a shame, because they're as incredible as they were when I brought you here for Valentine's Day when we were in high school. Back then, I'm pretty sure you ate more than me." He picked up a berry. "I guess I'll get to make up for that this time."

Jessica watched him eat the second berry, again enjoying every bit. She could smell the sweet fruit, see how juicy the berries were by the way he licked his lips between each bite.

She waited until he closed his eyes in his enjoyment and then slid the plate to her side of the table. "You're going to have to wait a second. I'm two behind." And she made him watch her eat two amazingly delicious berries. "Oh, my, they're just as good as I remembered."

Smirking, Chad reached for the plate, slid it back to the middle of the table. "Are you willing to share the rest?" he teased.

"Do I have to?"

He laughed. "And I wasn't sure whether that memory was correct, that you actually did outeat me that night."

"Hey, they're good," she countered, but she indicated the remaining berries. "But I'll share this time."

They finished the remaining strawberries, then Chad paid for dinner and they left the restaurant. Once again, he opened her door, and once again, Jessica felt a sense of giddiness as she sat in the car. There was something heady about being pampered by Chad Martin.

Who was she kidding? There was something heady about simply being near Chad Martin.

When he slid into his seat, she was laughing.

"What?" he asked.

"I'm just…happy." That was the best and simplest way to describe it.

He smiled. "I'm glad. I'm happy, too, happier than I've been in a very long time." He moved the keys toward the ignition but then paused. "Jess."

Her laughter was still subsiding, but she swallowed the last of it when she saw his face. He'd turned toward her, and those green-gold eyes were filled with emotion. Love, Jessica thought, but also something else. Something almost…sad. "Chad, what is it?"

"A lot happened in the years we were apart," he said, examining her face as he spoke. "I really don't think you can understand how much this, how much you mean to me unless you know what I went through while we were apart." He ran his hand through his hair and then glanced at his hand. Shaking his head, he eyed the gold band. "I can't believe I forgot to take it off." Then he slid the wedding ring from his finger and dropped it in his shirt pocket. "Sorry."

"It's okay." It was okay. Jess knew why he wore the ring when he was teaching, since he'd explained that on the first night they ran into each other on campus. But she wasn't certain that he was merely apologizing for the ring. The look on his face said that maybe he was saying he was sorry about whatever he went through while they were apart.

"I need to tell you what all happened. Need to tell you about Kate and about Lainey." He paused a couple of beats, then said, "If we're going to be together, and I want that more than you can realize, then I don't want there to be anything you don't know."

Jessica swallowed. God was helping her out by having Chad share his past with Kate. Then she could share her past, too. "I want to tell you, too, about everything that happened to me while we were apart. And about Nathan."

He nodded. "Let's go to the park. We've got a lot

to talk about, and we can enjoy the Valentine's display while we do." He smiled. "Sound okay?"

"Yes, that sounds great," she said. And it did. They would be at the park, decorated for the holiday, in an atmosphere that embodied love and relationships, when she told him about his son. It was more than great.

It was perfect.

Hydrangea Park was only a ten-minute drive from the restaurant, and Jessica saw the pink, red and white illumination well before they reached the entrance of the park. Thousands of tiny lights adorned every tree, bush and fixture that composed the park. The entrance consisted of two mature pecan trees, the branches meeting in the center to form a welcoming arch. But during the Valentine's display, the branches, barren of leaves during the winter, were covered with red lights that dangled in the center to form a heart.

They drove between the trees and parked the car. Jessica didn't make an effort to climb out until Chad opened her door, which caused him to smile. She was glad for that smile. He'd seemed so serious at the restaurant's parking lot when he'd mentioned the years they were apart. Obviously, there was a tremendous amount of pain and hurt in his years.

She was ready to learn what had happened to Chad, and she was ready to tell him the truth about her years away from him as well.

"That gazebo is open," he said, indicating the white structure, practically glowing with tiny pink lights, near the pond. "Want to go there and talk?"

"Sure," she said, climbing out of the car, then shivering. A light breeze blew across the pond, and the temperature was dropping in time with the sun dipping behind the mountains.

Chad noticed and leaned in his car to withdraw a navy blazer from the backseat. "It'll be big on you, but it should keep you warm." He helped her put it on, lifting her loose strands of hair out of the way as he did and sending a frisson through Jessica's senses that had nothing to do with the cold.

He turned her to face him, drew the jacket together and then gently pulled the lapels to slowly bring her face mere inches from his. "You're beautiful," he whispered.

Then, while Jessica lost herself in the combination of his words and her desire for this incredible man, he eased closer and brushed a feather-soft kiss against her lips. The tender touch echoed through her very being, sending delicate waves of awareness to her soul.

I love you. I've always loved you. I've never stopped loving you. I love you, and I love our son.

The words tumbled over her thoughts, the truth of her feelings, and the yearning for a lifetime of moments like this.

Without saying a word, he took her hand and led her toward the gazebo. A garland of pink roses covered the chains holding a white wooden swing in the center of the circular structure.

They stepped inside, and Jessica was surprised at the instant difference in temperature. Even though the sides were primarily open, with an intricate lattice wall providing the only separation between the interior and outside, the fixture warded off the majority of the breeze. The space was warm and comfortable. Oddly enough, even with several other couples also wandering around the park to enjoy the romantic display, the gazebo was startlingly private. The perfect place to have an intimate conversation.

For a moment, they sat in silence on the swing. It creaked softly as they moved back and forth, the scent of the pink roses more prominent as the garland shifted with each movement. The air grew thicker around them, as though all of the words defining their years apart joined them in the small space. Everything they needed to say, needed to explain, weighed down upon their souls. Jessica could feel the pressure of this moment and didn't underestimate the importance of telling Chad the truth.

Now that she'd made up her mind to have the conversation, Jessica was eager. She wanted him to know about Nathan, and she wanted him to meet his son. Yes, it would be difficult at first, but she hadn't missed the way Chad had looked at her tonight or the feelings that were right there, so easy to acknowledge with his words and with his touch. He still loved her just as she still loved him. And though he might be disappointed in her for keeping Nathan from him, he would want them all to be together, to be a real family. Jessica was sure he would want that as much as she did.

"Chad, I need to tell you…everything," she said, her heart racing faster with every word. "About why I left back then and about what happened after I did. I want you to know about Nathan."

"Jess, wait," he said. "I've been thinking about this all day, all week, and I definitely want to know why you left, but I'm afraid if I don't say this now I may not ever say it." He shook his head. "It isn't easy to admit how much I was fooled by my ex. In fact, I've never told anyone the entire story. But for you to understand what you mean to me—and why you mean so much to me now—I need you to know what happened."

Not only could Jessica hear the agonized pain in his tone but she could see it in his eyes. What had happened to him to hurt him that much? And she couldn't help but wonder what he meant by saying that knowing what happened would help her understand how much she means to him now. She did want to tell him about her years away. She truly wanted to tell him about Nathan. But she could tell that his truth was also torturing his soul, and he needed to tell her first. "Okay."

"You said Becky told you that I'd married," he said.

"She did." His sister had actually told her a few days before Chad's wedding, when Jess had returned to Claremont to tell him about Nathan. After learning about the impending wedding, she'd returned to Tennessee without telling him anything.

He took a deep breath, eased it out. "It took me a long time to get over you leaving, Jess. I went to Georgia and pretty much got consumed with becoming a doctor. I studied nonstop, got my premed degree in three years and then started at Emory. I didn't date, not once, throughout those first years at Georgia. But after I graduated, and after I moved to Atlanta, I met Kate. She worked at the hospital as an office assistant, and I met her at the corporate picnic. I still remember how interested she was in my plans, how she truly seemed interested in me."

"Women are naturally interested in you," Jessica said, smiling. "You just don't tend to notice."

He smiled at that, and she was glad to get a smile out of him. She could tell this conversation wasn't easy.

"Kate and I dated a year, and during that year, we couldn't see each other enough. I'd been on my own for so long and hadn't even realized how much I missed being with someone, caring for someone...and having someone care for me."

Jessica swallowed thickly. She'd been the reason he'd been alone and the reason he'd had to miss someone caring for him during that time. She had cared for him, thought of him, each and every day they were apart, particularly when she looked at their son, but he hadn't known.

"I fell for her—" he paused "—fell in love with her, pretty fast, and that December, I asked her to marry me. I was busy in med school, naturally, but she didn't seem to mind. She was also busy, planning the big wedding and the honeymoon. She started making friends with the doctors' wives at the hospital, even though I was still in school. She wanted her place in the medical society to be ready for her when the time came." He shrugged. "At the time, I thought that was cute."

Jessica didn't know what to say to that, so she remained silent and let him sit for a moment gathering his thoughts.

"After the wedding, when she didn't have anything to plan, Kate wasn't happy with the long hours I spent in class or studying. I spent every moment I could with her. I loved my wife, and I wanted her to be happy. But she couldn't stand the thought that she was working full-time while I was taking out student loans to get through med school. She said she was working herself to death while I 'merely went to class.' So I got a job working in a pharmacy on campus."

"Which meant you had even less time together," Jessica reasoned.

He nodded. “She’d loved the idea of being a doctor’s wife. She just wasn’t so crazy about being a med student’s wife.” He chuckled, but there was no humor in the sound.

“I’m sorry, Chad,” Jess said, and she slid her hand across the swing to lay her palm on top of his. “That had to be hard.”

He visibly swallowed. “What was hard was receiving a phone call from her best friend, all worked up and in a frenzy because she thought I should know that Kate was pregnant.”

Jess tried to put that together. “Her friend told you that you were having a baby? Kate didn’t tell you?”

Chad’s head shook slowly. “No, and the only reason I found out from her friend was because Phoebe thought I had a right to know that my—” his voice broke “—that my wife had decided to end her pregnancy and was headed to an abortion clinic.”

Jessica gasped and immediately saw Lainey, her beautiful blue eyes, soft blond curls and sweet, innocent smile. “Oh, Chad!”

His jaw was firm and tense, mouth was a straight line. The ache in his soul was palpable. “I’ve never driven so fast in my life, trying to get there in time to stop her.”

“But you did stop her,” Jessica whispered, again thinking of adorable little Lainey and the way she smelled like baby shampoo and the way she loved to be read to. And the way she felt, snuggled up close and sleeping in Jessica’s arms.

“I begged her, with everyone there watching me cry. I begged her not to give up our child. I begged her not to take that baby away from us, away from me.” His mouth rolled in, and he bit his lip. “She screamed at me then, said she didn't want the baby and that she no longer wanted me and all of my schooling."

Jessica shook her head, disbelieving that anyone could be so hateful, so cruel. So willing to end a life. "How did you stop her?"

"I told her nothing mattered, not school or my career or my dreams or anything, as much as Kate and our child. I promised her I'd quit med school and get a job that would put me at home more with her and the baby. I told her I'd teach or something else—anything that would make her happy and make her want the baby." He paused, swallowed. "And me."

Jessica moved closer to him on the swing. Her tears burned as they pressed forward and fell onto her skirt. Chad had been through so much and had given up so much for his wife and child. But Jessica knew that he would have done anything,—anything—for his wife and for his child. Especially after growing up the way he did, without his father, and seeing his mother struggle through raising him and Becky. Like he had vowed in high school, he had married for life. For better or worse, Chad had married for life.

Yet he and Kate still divorced. Now Jessica wondered even more…why?

"She told me in that clinic that she didn't want to be a mother, at all," he said, his voice raspy and raw. "Even though we'd talked about having kids the entire time we were dating, she didn't want to go through having to care for a child. So I promised her I would get up at night, that I'd take care of the baby's needs, that I'd do everything if she wouldn't give up our child. With all of those promises, Kate finally relented and said she would continue the pregnancy. And seven months later, Lainey was born." His face lit up when he said his daughter's name. "I was probably stupid for thinking that once Kate saw the baby she'd change."

"But she didn't."

He shook his head. "I was thrilled with Lainey, her blue eyes and blond hair. She looked, well, she looked just like Kate. And she was a part of us, a product of the bond we had shared before Kate decided that she didn't want to be a part of 'us' anymore. I was hoping that Lainey would help Kate see that we were good together and that we'd created something good together."

"Holding Lainey, seeing Lainey, didn't cause her to bond with her?" Jessica asked and couldn't hide her shock. She had bonded with Lainey in the short time she'd known the adorable little girl. How had the child's own mother not been as drawn to her as everyone else?

"No," Chad said. "There was no bonding at all. Kate resented the baby and the time she required. She was miserable and didn't mind telling me so, continually. It didn't matter that I took the bulk of caring for the baby or that I took the teaching position at the community college here so that Mom could help out. In fact, Mom came over almost daily so that she could not only help take care of Lainey but also clean the house, cook, everything she could do to help me keep Kate content."

"Your mother knew about what happened?"

"I had to tell her because she'd known how much med school meant to me and needed to know why I was giving it up."

"And when you told her?"

"Oh, I know she was disappointed in Kate, but she never said one negative thing. If I made the decision to stay married to her, then she made the decision to support the marriage, too. Of course, I don't know what she would have done if Kate would have actually gone through with the abortion. But thankfully I'll never have to find out. I mean, if I hadn't gotten there in time—" he shook his head "—I can't imagine life without Lainey."

Jessica blinked back tears. "Of course you can't."

"Everything seemed like it was going okay for a while, thanks to Mom coming over as much as she could and Kate basically not having to do a thing for her child. And some part of me still hoped that maybe after the diaper stage or maybe when Lainey was a little bigger and could feed herself then Kate would come around. I'd heard that some women just didn't care for the whole baby stage but they loved having toddlers. I guess I hoped that might be the case for Kate. But then Lainey got colic. It was bad. She cried a lot, and she wouldn't sleep. We tried everything, all of the medicines that should have worked. None did. We drove her in the car, put her in her baby carrier on top of the dryer, rocked her, held her close, you name it."

Jessica remembered Nathan's problem with colic and how she felt like she was spending nearly every penny she earned on the Mylicon drops that settled his aching tummy. It was worth every one of those pennies to help him feel better, and thankfully those drops did help. She also remembered how much it upset her to see him hurting and hear him cry.

"One night, her colic was worse than it'd ever been, and she screamed for a solid hour. Kate and I had already been arguing that night." He shrugged. "I don't even remember what we were fighting about, but when Lainey was in my arms, her stomach so tight it felt like a hard ball against my side, and when she was screaming her tiny lungs in my ear, Kate screamed something, too. She yelled out the truth about the baby in my arms."

"The truth?" Jessica asked, bracing herself for what he was going to say and fearing that it was even worse than what Chad had already told her.

Her fears came true with Chad's next words.

"She told me that Lainey wasn't mine." Thick, heavy tears fell down his face.

Jessica's heart clenched in her chest, his anguish riveting through her as he relived the horrific pain Kate's words inflicted.

"She said that Lainey wasn't mine, that she didn't want Lainey and that she didn't want me. Then she told me that she'd met a doctor—a real doctor—and they were in love."

"Oh, Chad." Jessica slid closer to him, her side against his, and attempted to transfer the depth of her compassion to his soul. "I'm so sorry."

He looked straight ahead, as though looking at Jessica would push his anguish over the brink and he might not be able to finish telling her what happened. "After the divorce, I didn't want to go back to med school. The required hours would have kept me away from Lainey too much. She'd already lost her mother, I wasn't about to make her lose me, too. So I kept working at the college and taking care of Lainey." He paused, and his mouth relaxed into a soft smile. "I love my little girl, regardless of the fact that we don't share the same blood. In my heart, she's mine, and I'll take care of her until the day I die."

"I know you will."

He shifted toward Jessica, turned the hand touching hers so that their palms met and their fingers automatically intertwined. Then he looked directly into her eyes, into her soul. "I wanted you to know about what happened with Kate because that's the only way you can understand how much this means to me. How much *you* mean to me, Jess. I loved you in high school, but I've learned so much since then about people and relationships." He gave her hand an affectionate squeeze. "You were good, the best person I'd ever known. Not only were you my best friend and the person I trusted with all of my most heartfelt feelings but you were the first girl I ever gave my heart to." He looked at the wooden floor of the gazebo and the corners of his mouth dropped. "Jess, you were truthful and honest, every moment of our time together. Even on the day you left, when you told me how you couldn't stay in Claremont after what we'd done, that you couldn't live with the fact that we gave in to temptation." He paused. "I know that was hard for you to say, hard for you to do, but you did it. I didn't want you to go," he whispered. "It tore me apart. Even more because I knew it was my fault."

Jessica's throat clamped shut. She attempted to swallow, but couldn't make it happen. She hadn't been honest back then; she'd lied. On that last night together, she'd said she couldn't live with what they'd done, but the truth was that she was still living with the reality of that one time together, when they let their desires take control. Still living—and loving—their son.

"Chad, no, you don't understand. I need to tell you…"

"I do understand, Jessica." Those green-gold eyes glistened with tears barely contained. "I understand how much your honesty means, how much it says about you that you want to do the right thing, even when it hurts. I know that when you say something, you mean it. When you do something, it's because you're convicted to your very soul." He cleared his throat, swallowed. "I trust you, Jess. I did back then, and I do now. After what happened with Kate, I truly didn't think I'd find that ability again, to believe in someone, to trust someone, to love anyone again."

"Chad, I need to tell you something."

"Okay, but let me finish first. I need you to know." His voice was warm, tender. "I loved you back then, Jess, but after being hurt so much, I realize just how lucky I am to have someone I can not only love completely but also trust with every ounce of my being. Lies and deception have no place in a relationship, and once you've been in one that's consumed by both, you appreciate the beauty of one that is consumed by truth and love." He brought his hand to her face, brushed the backs of his fingertips down her cheek to wipe away her tears. "I don't know if I could have ever given my heart again to anyone—but you."

The tears continued to press forward, and Jess simply couldn't speak. He could only give his heart to a woman he trusted, and she'd lied to him. For six years.

He edged closer, his face moving to hers as he spoke. "Don't cry, baby. Please," he whispered, his mouth against her cheek as he kissed away her tears. "Tell me now, Jess. I need to hear it, because I know from you it will be true."

Jessica's mind reeled. He wanted her to tell him? Now? How could she tell him the truth now?

He kissed her, softly, tenderly. Truthfully. Then he

looked into her eyes, straight into her soul, and asked again. "Tell me, Jess."

She swallowed, opened her mouth to speak.

"Tell me that you love me."

Jessica knew she should say more, much more than what he'd requested. She should give him everything he deserved, the truth of what had happened back then and the truth of the little boy with eyes just like his. But she couldn't. Instead, she gave him the only truth he'd asked for, and something she could say honestly, without a doubt, for eternity.

"I love you."

Chapter Ten

Jessica's father entered the kitchen, grabbed his favorite mug and poured himself a large cup of coffee. He then took a bright yellow mug with a smiley face on the side out of the cabinet and poured another cup. As usual, he left his black, but he added a healthy dose of French vanilla cream and sugar to the second cup. Then he brought both to the table and slid the happy-faced one toward Jessica.

"Thought you could use a smile."

"Thanks, Dad." She'd been sitting in front of a bowl filled with orange slices ever since her mother and Nathan had left for Walmart. This was the first glimpse she'd had of her father today, since he'd left early this morning to go fishing with one of the men from church, but Jessica had no doubt her mother had filled him in on what happened last night.

Jess couldn't sleep after Chad brought her home, and when her mother got up for her traditional two o'clock glass of water, she found Jess crying on the couch. After an hour of sharing what she'd learned about Chad and allowing her mother to hold her while her tears subsided, Jessica finally fell asleep on the sofa.

Which was where Nathan found her bright and early this morning proclaiming he wanted to go buy plenty of bread to feed the ducks at the park. He'd also reasoned that while they were out, they could get his new Superman pencils and notebooks. Thankfully, her mother had offered to take him, giving Jess a little time to prepare for the rest of the day, which she prayed would be better than she anticipated.

"So," her dad started, then took another sip. "Chad's been through a hard time."

A major understatement.

"Yes, sir."

Her mother had definitely filled him in, which was good. Jess didn't want to go through the whole thing again. She didn't think she could.

She allowed herself a swallow of coffee. The oranges her mother had placed before her hadn't been all that appealing, but the coffee was actually soothing. Warm and rich and sweet, exactly what she needed. Somehow, her dad had known.

"Enough cream?" he asked.

"It's just right."

He gave her a sympathetic smile. "Want to talk about it? I mean, do you want to talk to me about it?" His mouth edged to the side, the way it always did when he was pondering the exact words he wanted to say. "Your mother told me about his little girl, that she isn't his biological child. And she told me about everything his wife, or rather his ex-wife, put him through." His head shook slightly as he spoke, as though he couldn't believe it all either. "Don't know how some people can be so mean-spirited."

Mean-spirited. An accurate way to describe the woman who had ripped Chad's heart into pieces and destroyed his ability to trust anyone—but Jessica.

A low, guttural moan filled the kitchen, and Jess realized it'd come from her. She moved her hands to her forehead, pushed away her hair and rubbed her temples. "Daddy, what am I going to do? He's going to know. The minute he sees Nathan, he'll know. And we're taking Nathan and Lainey to the park—" she glanced at the clock on the stove "—in four hours. I'm the only woman he thinks he can trust. He said so. It's going to kill him when he finds out what I've kept from him."

His mouth moved to the side again, and once more, he paused to think through what he wanted to say. Jessica started to think he wasn't going to offer any additional conversation on the dismal subject, but then he asked, "Have the two of you ever talked about Nathan? Did Chad ask you anything about who his father is?"

"We were going to talk about that last night. We'd decided to tell each other everything about the years that we were apart, and last night seemed the perfect opportunity to do that. Chad said it was important for me to know about what happened to him so I could understand how he felt about relationships now."

"I think he's right about that. He's been through a lot and has shown himself to be strong through the storm. And Jess, it truly touched my heart how much he loves his daughter, regardless of her paternity. I've always thought a lot of Chad, but that proves that my judgment of his character was correct. He's a good man."

"I know." She sipped the coffee and again found it a

little easier to talk after feeling the warm, sweet taste on her tongue. "And he kept telling me how he wanted me to understand how much it meant to him that he could trust me."

"And after he told you about everything he'd been through and how he'd been deceived," her father deduced, "you decided you couldn't tell him about Nathan."

She blinked several times, trying to keep the tears at bay. She knew how much it hurt him to see her cry. He'd never been able to stand seeing her cry. "How could I tell him that I'd lied to him about something as important as his child, after he'd been lied to so much already? And after he'd just admitted that I'm the only woman he could ever trust with his heart."

"But you both said you would tell each other about the past last night. Wasn't he expecting you to tell him about your son?"

"Yes, but I was so upset about what Kate put him through, and about the way that he learned that Lainey wasn't his, that I told him my past could wait. I said we'd been through enough emotional turmoil for one night, and I didn't want any more sadness added to our time together."

"Which was true. You two obviously went through a lot together last night just in facing Chad's ordeal."

"Yes, but I'm not certain that's why I waited." She'd been battling the real fact about why she hadn't talked to him throughout the night, and she knew that she wouldn't lie to her father about it. "It wasn't because we'd discussed so much of his pain. There wasn't any reason for me to wait. I should have told him. I was stalling because I didn't want to tell him the truth."

He sipped his coffee, placed the mug back on the

table. "Honey, you do want to tell him the truth. That's why you're hurting so badly now. You want to tell him more than anything. What you don't want to do is hurt him."

She couldn't hold back the tears any longer, and they pushed forward and dripped onto the table by her cup. Jessica reached for the mug, wrapped her hands around it and completely covered the smiling face. Then she forced herself to take another sip. The liquid was still sweet but was growing cold, and she put the cup back on the table.

His mouth flattened, and she could tell he was working hard to control his own emotions. He was being strong, the way fathers knew they were supposed to be strong, even though Jess suspected that his heart was aching as much for her situation as her heart ached for Chad's. He released a deep breath and stood, moved to the kitchen counter and picked up his worn Bible. "You know, when your mother and I were married, the preacher at our wedding read to us from First Corinthians 13," he said, "the chapter of love."

Jessica watched as he thumbed through the pages and found the passage.

"When you listen to these verses, in theory, it all sounds pretty easy. But in practice, some of them can be rather tough." His finger guided down the page until he found the part he was looking for. "Love is patient, love is kind. It does not envy, it does not boast, it is not proud. It is not rude, it is not self-seeking, it is not easily angered, it keeps no record of wrongs. Love does not delight in evil but rejoices with the truth. It always protects, always trusts, always hopes, always perseveres."

Jessica immediately knew the portion of the passage

that he was referring to—the part that was tough, particularly for her now. "Love rejoices with the truth." She rubbed her thumbs over the wide smile on her cup and held them at the edges so that the grin became a frown. And the face looked more…like she felt. "I should have told him the truth last night. Putting it off is only going to make it harder, only going to make it worse."

"I'm sure it wasn't easy at that moment, after learning how deceived he'd been in the past. But Chad loves you, and you love him." His eyes moved back to the Bible and he repeated, "It always protects, always trusts, always hopes, always perseveres."

"But he did trust, and I've betrayed that trust."

"Love always perseveres," her father said softly. "It keeps no record of wrongs."

"But he doesn't even know about what I did. There isn't a record because I've never told him." She was expressing every concern that had haunted her through the night, yet her father wasn't swayed, ever determined to help her through a rough patch.

"You know, Nathan asked me to sing one of the songs from his Bible class with him last night before he went to bed. The one about the wise man building his house upon the rock."

Jessica managed a smile. "He loves that song, especially when the foolish man's house goes splat."

Her father grinned. "I noticed. He screamed that part."

"He likes to do that," she said, visualizing Nathan slapping his hands together and yelling through the chorus.

"Well, if you think about that song, it really applies to most every aspect of life, don't you think?" He cleared his throat. "One house was built on the rock, and the other was built on the sand. When the storm came, the house on the rock stood firm. The house on the sand fell flat."

Jessica nodded, hearing Nathan's sweet voice singing the familiar song.

"But, honey, the important part is that both houses had to endure the storm." He closed his Bible, looked at her thoughtfully. "Nothing about life is easy, and love definitely isn't. Everybody, every love has to weather the storms. Just because that wise man built his house on the rock didn't mean he wouldn't go through tough times. The storm still came."

"But his house was built on a rock. It was on a firm foundation. Right now, my foundation—the foundation of my love with Chad—is on shaky ground. We're on the sand, and I'm afraid we're going to fall."

"Love perseveres," her father repeated. "You have to believe that. It isn't too late to strengthen that foundation. I know it won't be easy, but anything worth having is worth a bit of effort. Your love for Chad and the chance for you, Chad, Lainey and Nathan to be a real family is worth working on that foundation."

"It's worth telling him the truth," she whispered.

"Yes." He took his mug, then picked up hers and took them to the sink. "You've already made up your mind to tell him, though, haven't you?"

"I made up my mind about that the day Nathan was born," she admitted. "I wanted Chad to know his son, and I wanted Nathan to know his daddy. But then he fell in love with someone else, married someone else. And I didn't know when the right time would be to tell him the truth. I knew I still wanted to tell him, but I just didn't know when."

"How did you plan to figure that out?" he asked, rinsing the mugs and putting them in the dishwasher.

"I guess I thought God would help me to know. I prayed for Him to let me know. But what if I missed the time that I was supposed to tell him?" She turned the bowl of oranges as she spoke.

"What do you mean?" he asked.

"I nearly told Chad last night. Everything was right for me to tell him. He'd told me the truth about his past, even though it hurt him terribly to tell me, and then he'd expected me to tell him about mine. But I didn't. I put it off." She continued to turn the bowl, the orange slices shifting slightly as it moved. A short while ago, the pieces had all been together, one part of a whole. Complete. Now they were separate and couldn't fit back together again. What if once Chad's trust in her was broken it couldn't be restored?

"You can tell him today," he said. "It may have been God's plan for you to tell him today, with Nathan by your side."

Jessica wasn't so sure. She'd felt certain she was supposed to talk to Chad last night, and she'd ignored the opportunity because she'd been afraid. Yes, she would see Chad in a few hours and would have no choice but to tell him, since he was bound to see the resemblance between himself and his son. But still…that didn't seem like the right thing to do. What would he say when he realized the truth? And wouldn't that be cruel, putting him in a situation where he couldn't tell her how he really felt about her keeping the truth from him because he wouldn't want to say anything in front of Nathan?

He wouldn't want to hurt his son.

"I don't think that was God's plan," she said. "I think that was my plan, to try to make it easier on me."

Her father's cell phone rang, and he withdrew it from his pocket and glanced at the front. "It's your mom." He pushed Talk. "Hi, honey. You and Nathan having a good—"

Jessica knew her dad well enough to notice the instant that his tone changed. Moreover, she caught the way his hand tightened on the phone and how his brows drew together and his body tensed.

Something was wrong.

Her father was a pillar, the one who held it all together in the worst of times. He was the sibling who was there for his brothers and sister when their mother passed on, the resilient one who held it all together throughout the funeral planning and then the emotional service…only to fall apart later at home. Jessica had heard him back then, his heart-wrenching sobs echoing from her parents' bedroom. But before then, when he'd been meeting with the funeral home, writing the obituary for the paper and notifying family and friends, he'd been a rock—a rock to the rest of the world, that is. Jessica had known the entire time that he was working hard to hold it together.

And back then, when he was fighting the emotional torture of losing some he loved, he looked…exactly like he looked right now.

"Mom," Jessica whispered. He'd looked at the phone and said it was her mother. Then he'd started talking and stopped, and now he had that look. That terrifying look. "What happened to Mom?"

Her father was still listening to the person on the other

end of the line, a person who Jess suspected was not her mother. Who had her mom's phone? And why?

The muffled echoes of the person's words weren't clear enough for Jessica to make out what the man was saying. But she was sure it was a man. The voice was deep and commanding, evidently informing—or maybe even instructing—her father about something. Something to do with her mother.

"No, I'm glad you got the phone and called. Thank you. And we'll leave right now."

Then it hit her. "Nathan." Nathan had been so excited about going to buy that bread and those pencils and notebooks. And her mother had been so nice to offer to take him since Jessica had such a rough night. But what if—what if they'd been in an accident? "Dad? Tell me what happened."

Her father closed his eyes and nodded to the voice on the other end of the line, his mouth clamped shut and his knuckles stark white as he clutched the phone. Finally, he disconnected, moved to the door and grabbed his keys from the wooden hook on the wall. "Come on, Jess. We've got to go to the hospital. They were in an accident, and they're both banged up. The guy who called saw everything and called 911."

She stood so fast her chair fell, but she didn't bother picking it up. At once she was by his side and hurrying out the door. "What happened?" she asked, fear radiating through her at the possibilities. "And what do you mean by banged up? What exactly happened?"

"They were in the turn lane, waiting to turn into the shopping center, when a guy ran a red light."

"He hit them?" Jessica jumped in the car, slammed her seat belt into place.

"Apparently, from what the guy on the phone said, he hit another car, and that car lost control and hit your mother and Nathan." He quickly backed out of the driveway, pressed the button for the flashers and started down the street. "Jess, he said your mother's going to be okay, that she has some cuts and bruises but that she was conscious at the scene. She gave this guy her phone and told him to call us, tell us to come to the hospital. She's… she's with Nathan." He swallowed thickly, his jaw tensing as he pressed the gas pedal to the floor.

"What about Nathan?" *Let him be okay. Please, God, let him say that Nathan is okay.*

"Jess, he's unconscious," he said, and a thick tear slid down his cheek with the words. "Evidently the back of the car spun around and hit a light post. Even with his seat belt on, he was jostled hard. Or that's what the guy on the phone said. We'll know more when we get to the hospital."

The back of the car spun around and hit a light post. The back of the car. Where Nathan, her precious little boy, was sitting.

Her father's phone rang again, and he handed it to Jessica. She didn't recognize the number but assumed it was someone from the hospital. *God, let him be okay. Please, please, God, let him be okay.*

"Hello."

"I was trying to reach Bryant," the voice on the other end said. "Is this—is this Jessica?"

She recognized Brother Henry's voice. "Yes, it's me," she said, barely aware that she was speaking, her senses were so consumed with fear for her son.

"Mary just called. She was coming home from shopping and thought she saw your mother's car—" he said, hesitating.

"They were in an accident," Jessica confirmed. "We're on our way to the hospital." Then she added, "Brother Henry, please pray for Nathan. He's—the back of the car was hit hard and he's unconscious. And I'm—I'm so scared. Please pray."

"I will," he promised. "And I'll call the phone tree. We'll have the entire church praying, and I'll meet you at the hospital. I'm leaving now." He disconnected and so did Jessica.

"He's calling the church to pray for him." A piercing sob pushed from her throat, and she couldn't stop the tears. "I can't lose him, Daddy. He's my world."

Her father pressed the pedal harder, and the car jolted through the familiar neighborhoods that now became a blur of houses, trees and sidewalks. Jess couldn't make them out at all through her tears. Her head started throbbing, pulsing against her eyes, and her stomach pitched, threatening to lose the only thing it held, that one cup of coffee.

"Oh, God, he's so precious. And he's so happy." Jess could see Nathan, telling her all about the notebook and pencils he was going to get and squealing about how much fun he was going to have at the park.

The park!

Chad.

Jessica's gasp was so loud that her father took his eyes off the road to see what was wrong.

"Jess! What?"

"He doesn't know. Chad doesn't know about Nathan and now...now Nathan's hurt...he's unconscious, and I don't know what's wrong. And Chad doesn't know. Oh, Daddy, what am I going to do?"

More thick tears slid down her father's cheeks. "Call him, Jess. You have to get him to that hospital. He needs to be there. Nathan is hurt. His son is hurt, and he should know. He should be there."

She pulled her phone out of her pocket while her father turned on the street leading to Claremont Hospital. The building ahead looked ominous and cold, not at all the type of place for a five-year-old boy. Not at all the type of place where Nathan should be. A huge red sign reading Emergency centered the entrance on their left, where her father steered the car. Her son was in that hospital, in that emergency room, and he was unconscious. Her son…and Chad's.

God, be with Nathan, she prayed. And then, pressing Send on the phone, she prayed, *God be with Chad, and please, dear God, be with me.*

Chad hadn't been with the guys since October, when their fall baseball season had ended. The men's team from Claremont was composed primarily of guys in their mid-twenties to early thirties. Young enough to remember how to play the game but old enough to know they weren't invincible. Case in point, Chad had thrown out his shoulder last spring, and he'd merely been warming up. He'd had to take a good deal of heat from them over that…until Mitch Gillespie broke his foot attempting to slide into second base. Then all the attention, jokes and "old man" terminology turned to Mitch. Guys would be guys.

The day was absolutely gorgeous, with enough of a breeze to keep them cool in spite of their exertion and enough warm sunshine to remind them that spring—and baseball games—were just around the corner. Which meant they needed this practice.

Practice, particularly the first practice of the season, for the team was extremely-low key. Mainly, they were getting the feel of the game again, working the muscles that hadn't been used nearly enough in the winter and attempting to burn off the extra pound or two that they'd accumulated during those Thanksgiving and Christmas meals. During a real game, they got down to business and concentrated on the main event. At this practice, however, they were more focused on having fun and catching up.

Chad listened as the ones who had kids talked about what their little guys and girls were currently doing, and he naturally joined in with Lainey's latest adventure of losing his phone. Then they all chatted about their wives or girlfriends, as the case may be. Chad didn't offer anything toward that conversation, thinking he'd merely wait and bring Jessica to meet the group when the time was right. But Claremont was too small a town for his secret to go unnoticed.

"Hey, Chad, Jana said she was sure she saw you last night when we were taking in the light display at Hydrangea," Mitch said, grabbing his glove from the bench and then taking a big sip of Gatorade before returning to the field. "I couldn't tell, but whoever it was in that gazebo had a really pretty brunette by his side and looked like he was having a fairly intense conversation with her."

Adam Finley, the third baseman and leadoff batter, heard the comment and cocked his head toward Chad. "That so? You found something serious, Martin?"

The group had played ball together and hung out

together since elementary school. They were friends and close enough that all of them knew that Chad hadn't been in any kind of real relationship since the downfall with Kate. Even if they didn't know exactly what had happened to end his marriage, they knew enough to know that he'd been burned and wasn't getting back into another serious relationship until he was certain that wouldn't happen again.

They didn't know the details about Lainey's paternity, and Chad certainly never planned to tell them. She was his, and that was all that mattered. But he also knew that these guys wouldn't mind seeing him happy. All of them had been lucky in love, either marrying their high school sweethearts or meeting someone in college, someone who actually cared about them and stayed with them. A few of their wives had naturally tried to fix Chad up over the last year, but nothing had worked out. He knew it was his problem, not theirs.

He had trust issues. He simply hadn't been able to trust his heart with anyone again. No one, that is, except Jessica. He'd told her the truth last night. She was the one who'd never let him down—his best friend and his first love. And, if he had his way, his last love.

The smile that took over his face didn't go unnoticed.

"All right, that does it. Who is she?" Adam asked. "All this time Lisa kept trying to find the right friend for you, and you already had someone in the wings?" Adam's wife had set Chad up with practically every female she knew, but none of them had set off any sparks, and none of them had even been introduced to Lainey.

"Actually, they were in the gazebo," Mitch said, laughing. "But Jana also thought you looked pretty intense, and I'd have to agree."

It was Chad's turn to bat, so he grabbed his favorite Louisville Slugger and headed for the plate. But John Cutter, the pitcher, had been listening to the conversation taking place in the dugout and stood on the pitcher's mound contently tossing the ball in his hand. "We're waiting on an answer, Martin," he called from the mound.

Chad heard Mitch laugh again. And to think, people thought women were the ones who fed on gossip. They obviously hadn't met his friends. "I wanted to bring her to the field sometime and let you figure it out on your own," he said. He'd actually envisioned Jessica, Lainey and her son in the stands cheering him on as he attempted to act like he was still in high school again. Maybe he wouldn't throw his shoulder out again in front of them.

"So we know her?" John still tossed the ball.

"It's Jessica," Chad said, and he knew there was no need for a last name. They'd all been together in high school, and when Chad's world ended during the spring of that senior year, when Jessica left Claremont, these were the guys who helped him pull through, often by bringing him out to the field and letting him work off his stress with a ball and bat. They'd continued playing together that year well after the high school's baseball season ended—not so much because they loved the game but more because Chad needed it.

"Jessica? Your Jessica? She's back?" Mitch asked, his dark brows disappearing beneath the bill of his cap as they shot upward.

His Jessica. That's the way it was back then, and that's

the way it was again. He smiled. "Yes, she's back, and that's who you saw me with in the gazebo."

A whistle sounded from the mound, and John Cutter bobbed his head as though everything made sense now. "Bowman is back. No wonder you're smiling. Never understood why you two split up or why she left," he said, not really to Chad but more to himself.

"Me, either," Mitch said. "And back then, you didn't understand it yourself. So, I'm assuming you finally found out what made her go, back then?" Mitch asked. "It'd better have been a good reason, for all the mess we had to go through that spring trying to get you to join the ranks of the living again."

Chad smirked. "And to think, I thought we were hanging out because we liked each other."

Mitch grinned. "Yeah, that was it. Anyway, I always thought something must've happened with her family, maybe they'd upset her somehow, but they always seemed pretty tight. I remember she went to live with her grandmother. Was that it? Was she sick or something?"

Chad rested the bat on his shoulder because obviously John had no plans of pitching to him in the near future. On the contrary, the entire team had moved in closer to hear all about what had happened to Jess way back then. He didn't blame them. He was a royal mess that spring and summer, and they really had worked hard to cheer him up. But there was no cheering him because he'd known why she left, and the problem had been…him. He was the one who hadn't stopped them from going further than they needed to on that one afternoon at his house. She had sensed them getting too close to the edge and had told him she should go home, but Chad

had encouraged her to stay. And she'd been right; they hadn't stopped.

Then she'd left town, unable to stay and live with what they'd done.

"We're still working through what all happened then," he said. Chad would give anything if he could go back and change the things that happened and caused her to leave, but he couldn't. However, he could make certain that now that she'd returned to Claremont—now that she'd returned to him—he'd never do anything to lose her again. And this time, he planned to follow through on those promises he made to her back in high school. He would marry Jessica Bowman, and he would marry her for life. "But she's back, and I'm planning on getting it right this time," he told them.

"Back in Claremont, you mean? For good? Are you sure?" Adam asked. Chad knew why he asked. His friends may try to act like they were tough guys, but every one of them knew how much he'd hurt when she left, and he knew Adam's questions were an attempt to make sure that didn't happen again. They were protecting their friend, and he appreciated them for it.

Chad nodded. "She's working on getting her teaching degree at Stockville. That's where we ran into each other. And until she gets her teaching degree, she's working as a teaching assistant at Lainey's day care. And her son is in kindergarten at Claremont." *And she's back with me.* He thought of the kisses they'd shared, and his heart warmed. He wanted many more kisses like that, many more moments like that, where he opened his soul and knew that everything he told her would be accepted with kindness, understanding and love. "I'd say she's intent on staying in town."

Chad had felt an inner peace last night after telling her about everything that happened with Kate. The sharing of that time in his life, letting her in on what he'd been through and on how much he'd been disappointed in his marriage—and in his wife—had brought him even closer to Jess. And he'd understood why she didn't feel comfortable talking about what had happened to her during their years apart and why Nathan's father hadn't married her. He assumed those years and the pain that guy inflicted hurt her as much as Kate's deception hurt him. And, as she'd said after he'd told her about Kate, they had been through enough pain for one night.

Chad did want to know what had happened, and he definitely wanted to know about Nathan's father. If Chad was going to assume a role in Jessica's son's life, then he wanted to know whether Nathan's biological dad still had any involvement with his child and to what extent. Jessica had said she would always love him, but she hadn't mentioned whether the guy was still around.

He sighed and wished that they could have discussed her past, too, last night. Like his, they would need to address her past in order to deal with their future. And he wanted to get to that future together…soon.

Chad had been so absorbed in his thoughts that he hadn't noticed the multitude of confused glances passing between the guys in the dugout and on the field. But John Cutter, always the most outspoken of the pack, wasn't going to let Chad's informative comment go without mention.

"She has a son?"

"His name is Nathan," Chad said. "I'm actually meeting him today. We're taking the kids to the park."

"She was married?" Adam asked, his bewilderment with this bit of news evident from his tone.

"No, she never married," Chad said, and before they pounded him with more questions he couldn't answer, he added, "And for now, that's all I know."

Mitch, now leaning against the chain link fence composing the dugout, brought his hand to his chin and rubbed it the way he always did when something stumped him. "That doesn't seem right." He shook his head.

Mitch was a year younger than Chad and had been in Jessica's grade in school. Therefore, he had been closer to Jess than Chad's other friends. In fact, Mitch had been a friend to both Chad and Jess before they'd even acknowledged their feelings for each other. He'd also been the one who, in ninth grade, informed Jess that Becky's brother wanted to know what she thought of him. Bottom line, Mitch knew Jessica pretty well, and the thought of her having a baby with a guy she wasn't married to apparently shocked him as much as it shocked Chad.

"That's all you know?" Mitch questioned. "She hasn't told you about his father? Or why she didn't marry him?"

"She's going to tell me," Chad said. "We were going to talk about it last night, but it didn't work out." He didn't feel the need to say anything more about their emotional discussion because he didn't want to get into his past with Kate again. It'd been enough to go through it last night with Jess. "But we're being honest with each other about our pasts, and she will tell me when the time is right," he said, for some reason feeling the need to explain why he didn't know more about the guy Jessica would always care for because he was the father of her son.

None of the guys said anything to that, and Chad suddenly wished that they would have continued talking last night and moved on to what happened to Jessica when they were apart. The fact was, she had a son, and therefore, she had a man who played a significant role in her life and would always play a significant role in her life because of the bond they shared. And Chad had no idea who the guy was or how large a role he'd play in his future with Jessica. Unlike Kate, Nathan's father could desire a strong presence in his son's life. And Chad would need to deal with that.

But Jessica had hardly mentioned him. Maybe he was like Kate after all. And if that was the case, then Chad would happily fill that void in little Nathan's life. He adored being a father to Lainey. He would adore being a father to Nathan, too, if everything worked out the way he wanted.

The silence from the guys on the field now was almost eerie, and Chad lifted the bat from his shoulder and tilted his head toward Cutter. "You going to throw the ball, or you just going to stand there all day?"

John grinned, tossed the ball in the air once more then assumed his pitching stance. "Guess you'll have a boy to bring to the park with you soon, huh?" he said.

Chad smiled. "Guess I will." Then he watched John wind up and throw his best fastball. Chad swung and knocked it to the fence. Rounding the bases wasn't all that necessary, since there wasn't a soul in the outfield where he'd hit the thing, but it felt good to run, and Chad enjoyed heckling the other guys as he passed each base. He made quite a production of crossing home plate, then cracked up laughing when Mitch slapped him on the back, way too hard to be considered congratulatory.

He entered the dugout on cloud nine. He would have a boy to bring with him to the field soon, Nathan. And he couldn't wait to meet Jessica's little guy, to introduce him to Lainey and then maybe tonight to spend more time with Jess and learn what had happened to her that had left her raising Nathan alone.

A little winded from base running, Chad grabbed his Gatorade from his bag and gulped down a nice portion of the bottle, then wiped his mouth with the back of his hand. He and Jess would spend time with the kids today, and then more time by themselves tonight. They'd talk, this time about her, and in the process they'd grow closer. And they'd continue to grow closer, the same way they always had every time they were together, and in the not-too-distant future, if everything went the way Chad hoped, he would marry the girl of his dreams and be a father of two. Lainey and Nathan.

He couldn't wait.

A buzzing noise caught his attention, and he saw that his baseball bag vibrated on the bench. He unzipped the bag, withdrew his cell phone and noted the new voice mail message displayed on the front. He quickly thumbed the keys to bring up the message and hoped that everything was okay with Lainey. She'd still been sleeping when he left for practice, and his mother already had her juice and pappy ready. Everything should have been fine.

Because Mitch was now batting, and the guys were consequently yelling and heckling, he had to cover his other ear in order to hear the frantic voice on the line.

But he did hear. And his heart clenched at the sound of Jessica so terrified.

"I've gotta go! Jessica's mother and Nathan were in an accident, and they're at the hospital," he yelled toward the field as he grabbed the bag and hurried from the dugout. "He's unconscious, and she wants me there."

"Go!" they yelled back as he sprinted for the car. He tossed his bag in, jumped in the driver's seat and then heard someone panting as they ran to catch up.

Mitch, his hand on his chest, stood beside the car. "Hey, man, Jana and I will get there as soon as we can and be with y'all. Tell Jessica that I'll pray for them."

Chad's gratitude was instant. Mitch hadn't talked to Jessica after she'd left six years ago. Chad knew that, but he obviously still cared about his old friend. And not only that but he cared about Chad. "Thanks." Chad slammed the car door and started the drive for the hospital, and he decided that even though he hadn't done it a lot lately, now was a good time to follow Mitch's lead… and he prayed.

God, be with Jessica's mom, and please be with her little boy. And help me to be there for her now and to say the right thing, do the right thing, to help Jess through this. Be with her son, Lord. And be with Jess.

Chapter Eleven

Jessica hadn't been able to reach Chad, so she'd left a message that didn't say a thing about him being Nathan's father. That just didn't seem like the type of thing you blurted into someone's phone. Plus, she knew Chad. She'd asked him to come, and he would come. When he got to the hospital, she'd let him know about Nathan. And she'd worry about how she'd handle that then. Right now, she simply needed to get to her son.

She and her father ran into the emergency room and were immediately met by a nurse who appeared to be waiting for their arrival. It took Jess a moment to place the lady. Typically, she only saw Maddie Farmer wearing dress clothes at church, but she now recalled that she worked as a nurse in the E.R. Jessica was instantly grateful to have a friendly face, and someone who would more quickly tell them what was going on at the hospital.

Maddie had definitely been watching for them and wasted no time steering them past the waiting area and through the large silver double doors leading to the back, where curtained rooms lined each wall.

"Your mom is in room three," she said. Then, directly

to Jessica's father, she said, "Anna is going to be okay, Bryant. Physically, she's only suffered a few scrapes and bruises. But she was in shock when she got here." She paused. "She's worried about her grandson."

"Where is he?" Jess asked, unable to control the volume of her tone or the panic in her voice. "Tell me, now, please!"

"He's still unconscious," the nurse said. "And they've taken him for some tests. We'll know more shortly, when the doctor returns. I promise I'll let you know as much as I can, as soon as I can." She slid back the curtain of room three, and Jess saw her mother, her head wrapped in a thick white bandage and a jagged cut down her right cheek. Tears streamed fluidly along the cut and down her throat, and her sobs became stronger when she saw them.

"Na-than," she whimpered. "How's Nathan?" Her teeth chattered nonstop, but she pushed the words through. "Is he—is he okay?"

Ms. Farmer moved to the IV beside the bed and adjusted the drip. "The doctors are taking care of him," she soothed, gently patting Anna's arm as she spoke, but her reassurance did nothing to help her spirits.

"Bryant, Jess," she said, still shaking in spite of the bounty of blankets Maddie piled on top of her quivering body. "Th-there was nothing we could do. The truck hit that car, and then the car, it j-just started spinning. Right at us." Her tears fell harder. "Like something out of a b-bad dream. Nothing to do but s-sit there and watch it happen. And Nathan," she said. "H-he screamed—" she looked at Jess "—for you." A sucking cry escaped her mother's lips, seeming to pull from her very soul, and Jessica's heart split.

Nathan had cried out for her when he was scared, when he was hurting. And now, he was unconscious, unable to cry out or scream or laugh…or look at her with those beautiful green-gold eyes.

Amazingly, until this point, Jessica had semi-held it together, but suddenly the reality of what had happened and what was happening now set in. She visualized her little boy on a flat table, with some kind of machine testing…what? His brain? Was that it? That had to be it, didn't it? He was unconscious, which obviously had something to do with his brain.

What if he woke up and he no longer remembered her? Or what if—what if he didn't wake up at all?

Her wail pierced through the rumble of nurses, doctors, patients and machines. It shrieked through the halls, echoed off the ceiling and at once, her legs gave way, the room blurred and everything disappeared.

Visions of Nathan, grinning with his cute little snaggletoothed smile and laughing at something she'd said, combined with visions of Chad, looking at her with those green-gold eyes and telling her he wanted a relationship with her, that he trusted her, that he loved her.

"I'm going to get lots of bread to feed the ducks," Nathan said, his hair standing on end from just waking up. His precious little face was a little fuzzy around the edges. Jessica tried to make it clear, but voices were getting in the way of her thought process. And then she thought she heard Chad's voice amid the flurry of sound. She focused on Chad, and suddenly she saw him, sitting beside her in the glowing gazebo.

"I loved you back then, Jess, but after being hurt so much, I realize just how lucky I am to have someone I can not only love completely but also trust with every

ounce of my being. Lies and deception have no place in a relationship, and once you've been in one that's consumed by both, you appreciate the beauty of one that is consumed by truth and love." He paused, then whispered, "She's coming back around."

Jessica didn't understand why his voice echoed so much within the gazebo, but she understood that this was the moment when she was supposed to tell him the truth, and she didn't want to mess that up again. She opened her eyes, and somehow she was no longer sitting by Chad. She was lying on her back, her head cradled in his arms, and he leaned over her, looking into her eyes.

"I'm here, Jess," he said, lovingly, tenderly.

"I'm so sorry I didn't tell you before," she said, and he leaned closer.

"I'm going to help you," he said. "You fainted, which is understandable, but you're going to be okay now. I'm here, and there's an entire waiting room of people here who care about you and who care about Nathan. Lots of people from the church are here. They're all praying for him."

Her mind jolted back to what had happened. They weren't in the gazebo, and she wasn't on that wooden, rose-covered swing. She was slumped in Chad's arms on the cold emergency room floor, where her son had been taken and where he was probably still being tested to find out why he wouldn't wake up. "Nathan," she said, then cleared her throat, shook her foggy mind. "Nathan! Where is he?"

"They're still doing the MRI," Chad said. "And Ms. Farmer has promised to let us know just as soon as we can talk to the doctor."

"When did you get here?" she asked, sitting up but knowing she wasn't quite ready to stand yet. Her head was heavy and pounded relentlessly.

"After I received your message, I got here as soon as I could, and I just happened to walk in the room in time to see you heading for the floor."

"You caught me," she said, vaguely remembering the feeling of falling, but not recalling the crash.

"Yeah, I did."

A plastic cup filled with water appeared in front of her face, and she looked up to see her father. "Here, honey."

She took the water, drank a long, cold sip. "How's Mom?"

"They gave her something to make her sleep for a little while. Hopefully, when she wakes up, she'll be past the shock. And maybe we'll have some good news to give her about Nathan by then."

"I want to see him."

"We told Maddie to let us know the minute we can be with him, and she promised she would," her dad said. "We're blessed that she was working today. She said she normally doesn't work on Saturdays but was filling in."

Jessica started to stand, and Chad wrapped a supportive arm around her as she did. They moved to a row of chairs nearby and sat, intensely watching the nurse's station for any sign of Ms. Farmer or anyone else who looked like they might know something about Nathan's condition.

"He needs me," she said. "Even if…even if he isn't awake, I'm sure he'll know that I'm there. I want to be there with him when he wakes up."

Her father exhaled thickly. "I know, honey, and I'm sure the doctor knows that, too. We just have to wait for them to finish what they're doing, and then I'm sure they'll let you see him." He glanced at Chad. "I'm glad you're here," he said. His mouth edged to the side, as though he were thinking whether to say something. Then he looked at Jess and didn't say anything else.

Because Jessica was the one who needed to tell Chad why her father was glad he was here, why it was so important for him to be here now, for his son.

"I'm going to check on your mom. Let me know if they come back with any news on Nathan." He walked away, then disappeared behind the curtain in front of room three.

"I know you're worried about Nathan," Chad said, "but the best thing we can do right now is to wait and see what the doctors say…and pray. I saw a small prayer room down the hall."

"I don't want to leave the emergency room until I hear about Nathan. We can pray here."

"I know, but the room is here, in the E.R.," he said, motioning toward a single door in the midst of the row of curtained entrances. "It will be a little quieter, and I'll let Ms. Farmer know where we are."

She nodded, listened to him tell Maddie Farmer where they would be then let him lead her to the door. Inside, like he'd predicted, it was quieter, without the beeping and buzzing of the machines in the E.R. units, the voices of nurses and doctors, and the sorrowful cries of the patients, their friends and families.

A single pew provided the only seating, and in front of the pew, a wooden cross centered the wall. On both sides of the cross, ornate stained glass gave the impression that the room had windows, even though they were completely enclosed within the E.R.

They sat on the pew and stared at the cross, and Jessica's eyes started to burn. God gave His son to die on a cross, to save the world from sin, and suddenly, with her son just a few rooms away and unconscious, Jessica wondered…how? How had He done that, even for all of their sins? The thought of Nathan hurting sliced at her very soul.

The thought of losing him…

She couldn't control the tormented cry that filled the room, and Chad instantly pulled her to his side and wrapped an arm around her. "Pray for him," she begged. "Please, Chad, pray."

"God," he said, and Jessica bowed her head next to his. "Please be with Nathan. Help him to be strong and to overcome…whatever is wrong, dear Lord. Be with the doctors who are caring for him, lay your hands upon them and guide them as they work to heal Jessica's little boy. He means the world to her, God, you know that. And be with her, too, Lord, so that she can be strong through the next few hours, days, however long it takes for Nathan to find his way back to her. And please, God, help him come back to her and to everyone who loves him so much. In Jesus' name, amen."

Jessica raised her head, looked at the cross, then looked at Chad. "Thank you."

"Jess, I haven't prayed near as much as I should have over the past few years, but I still believe He listens when I do."

"I believe He does, too." She sniffed, wiped fresh tears from her cheeks. "I need to tell you something, Chad, about Nathan, about his father. I should have told you before now, I know I should have, but I couldn't." She shook her head. "No, that's not true. I just didn't, and I'm sorry. I'm so sorry."

She noticed his cheeks were wet. "I don't know what to say to you," he said softly, his words barely heard in spite of the silence in the room. He didn't look at Jess but rather looked at the cross as he spoke. "I can only imagine what you're feeling, and I hurt for you. I haven't even gotten to meet Nathan yet, and still I hurt. I keep thinking about, well, if it were Lainey that we were waiting to hear about. And I do understand why you haven't told me about Nathan's father, how difficult that would be, but if we're going to be together, then he will obviously be a part of it, because he's a part of Nathan. And he should be here now. If you're comfortable telling me who he is, I'll call him, make sure he gets here to be with you through all of this."

He wiped his hand down his face, calming his emotions while also rubbing away his tears. "But I promise you, Jess, once we're together, Nathan will have a father around, always. I might not be his biological daddy, but that won't matter. I promise. He'll be mine, like Lainey is mine."

This was it. God was giving her the opportunity to tell him, right here—right now. And he needed to know, now, because Nathan needed both of his parents here to see him through this—right here, right now. They'd prayed together and now they needed to be there, together, to help their son.

God, help me tell him.

Jessica looked toward the cross and her father's words, the words from the chapter of love whispered through her thoughts. *It keeps no record of wrongs... love perseveres.*

"Chad, when I left six years ago, it wasn't because of what we'd done. I mean, it was, but not the way I made it seem. And you need to know the truth."

"Jess," he said, taking his hand to her chin and tenderly turning her face toward his. "You don't have to explain now. We can talk about it another time, and what matters is now, our future and Nathan."

"I know," she said. "That's why I have to tell you. Do you remember the last time I saw you back then?"

He nodded, but he looked at her as though he didn't understand why she'd bring this up now. In a moment, though, he would.

"I'd come to your house to see you, and you said you had some news, remember?"

Again, he nodded. "It was the night I got the scholarship to Georgia. I was so excited, and I told you all about it and how nothing would change between us."

"And then I went home and called you, told you that I was leaving, that I couldn't live with the fact that we'd given in to temptation that one time."

His eyes looked pained from the memory, and she hated that, hated that she'd hurt him so terribly with that lie. And hated that she was about to hurt him again.

But it was time for him to know the truth...for Nathan.

"When I came to see you that night, I had some news, too, but after I heard yours, I didn't tell you."

"What news, Jess?" Again, confusion etched his beautiful features, and Jessica pressed on. She had to.

"I didn't tell you because you were so excited about that scholarship, about your future and being a doctor and all, and I didn't want you to throw all of that away. And I knew you would."

He shook his head. "Jess, I'm not following you here. I think maybe you're still dazed from fainting earlier. Maybe I should go get someone to check you out." He started to stand, but she grabbed his arm.

"No, Chad, please. I have to do this. It's important that I tell you now. I—I've waited way too long."

"Okay," he said, still clearly perplexed at the conversation. He settled back onto the pew next to Jessica and faced her. "Tell me. Why would I have thrown everything away?"

"Because of my news," she whispered. "Because of the way you are, and the way you were brought up, and how much family means to you and how determined you were to always being there, to being—" she paused, swallowed and finally finished "—to being there for your child."

He looked at her, processed her words and Jess knew the moment he realized why she'd come to his house that night so long ago.

"He's yours, Chad. Nathan. He's yours."

His arm fell forward from the back of the pew. His mouth opened and his head moved, almost imperceptibly, from side to side in disbelief.

But he didn't say a word.

Jessica felt his body, ever so subtly, shift away from hers. She knew that he was dealing with the reality, with the possibility, of the truth. "I'm so sorry, Chad. I should have told you then, but I really thought I was doing what was best for you. I didn't want you to give up everything for me, and I knew you would."

His jaw tightened now, and he looked at her, the gold

in his eyes catching the light and dividing the seas of deep green with splinters of fire. “I would have. I would have given up the scholarship, the med school dream, everything to raise my child. Our child. And it would have been exactly what I wanted to do, because I never, ever wanted my child to grow up without me in his life. But that’s exactly what has been happening, isn’t it? My child, Nathan, hasn’t had a father. He hasn’t had me because you didn’t give me that chance.”

“I know, and I should have told you.”

“Yes, you should have.” He ran his hands through his hair, stood up and moved to the door.

“Where are you going?” she asked.

“I’m going to see my son.” He opened the door with Jessica close at his heels, and Jess saw Maddie point to her. The nurse beside Maddie hurried their way.

“Are you Nathan Bowman’s parents?” she asked.

“I’m his—” she started and then saw Chad’s eyes connect with hers and corrected the near error. “Yes, yes. We are.”

“Come with me. The doctor wants to see you.”

Chad and Jessica followed the woman down the back hallway, past the curtained rooms and past her father, standing by the closed curtain to her mother’s room.

“Jess? Chad?” he questioned.

“The doctor is going to talk to us about Nathan,” she quickly explained. “I’ll let you know what he says as soon as I can.”

Chad looked at her father as though wanting to say something or ask something, but then his mouth flattened and he continued following the nurse.

Jessica’s dad nodded at her, silently urging her to go on. And then he glanced at Chad, and she could tell that her father knew that she'd told Chad the truth. *Pray for us,* she mouthed, and he nodded again.

The back of the E.R. was much different than the front, more like regular hospital rooms, with pale blue walls and tall numbered doors marking each room.

"In here," the nurse said, opening a door to a small room with a couch, two chairs and a table. Obviously a room for patient consultation.

Jessica's stomach pitched. "What's wrong with him?" she asked the nurse.

"Dr. Aldredge is on his way," she said and gave Jess an apologetic smile. Was she sorry that she couldn't give Jess more information, or was she sorry about the condition of her—of their—son? She looked to Chad for his reaction, but he'd already taken one of the chairs and was staring at the door, as though willing the doctor to appear.

Jessica sat on the sofa, her entire being longing to see Nathan, to hold him. "I'm scared," she whispered.

"I'm scared, too," he finally said as the doctor briskly entered and took the other chair.

He shook their hands. "I'm Dr. Aldredge," he said and then sat in the other chair. "I know you're both anxious to see Nathan, and I'll let you, but I wanted to give you his current status. The good news is that the tests we've run so far show no physical or neurological damage. Nothing was apparent on our initial check or the CT scan, so we ran an MRI, which ruled out internal bleeding. And he's breathing on his own without any problems."

Chad leaned forward in his seat. "That's good."

Dr. Aldredge nodded. "Yes, it is. However, Nathan still hasn't regained consciousness, so we've moved him to a twenty-four hour monitored intensive care unit in our children's wing."

Jessica tried to grasp what he was saying but didn't know what to ask first. Thankfully, Chad did.

"Your diagnosis, then?" he asked, his voice appearing calm to anyone who didn't know him, but to Jessica, she could sense the underlying concern.

Dr. Aldredge shifted toward Chad. "From what I can surmise from the accident, the area where Nathan was sitting in the car received the brunt of the impact when the automobile collided with a light post. That external force jolted Nathan and apparently caused some form of traumatic brain injury."

Jessica gasped, her hand flying to her mouth, but Chad merely exhaled through his nose.

"The reason you say apparently is because he remains unconscious," Chad said, and the doctor nodded.

"Like I said, we haven't found any reason for Nathan not to wake up, and at this point, all we can do is watch him for the next twenty-four hours. After that, if we haven't seen any change, we'll potentially move him to Children's Hospital in Birmingham. However, it'd be best if we didn't have to move him, and for the time being, we're doing exactly what they would do if he were there." He tapped the clipboard in his lap and frowned. "I wish I could tell you more, but until his condition changes, there's nothing to tell."

"But we can see him," Jessica said.

"Yes. In fact, I'm a firm believer that it helps to have someone close by, talking to the patient, letting them know you're there, when they are unconscious. No one has proven that those who are unconscious are aware of anything around them, but no one has proven they aren't, either. There have been studies that lean both ways, but in my opinion, if it's a possibility, then it's worth a try."

"I agree," Chad said, rising from the chair. "So can we see him now?"

"Yes, of course." Dr. Aldredge led the way out of the room and down the hall, with Chad and Jessica following.

Jessica looked at Chad, saw the anxiousness in his demeanor. The doctor had no idea what Chad had asked, to see his son…for the first time.

"I'm so sorry," she whispered, softly enough that her words could only be heard by Chad.

"I am, too."

The walls changed dramatically with a turn down another hall, with colorful scenes from the Bible painted along every space. They went through the Garden of Eden, saw Moses with the Ten Commandments, then Noah's ark with an abundance of vivid animals. Dr. Aldredge moved to that door, put his hand on the handle.

"This area is for children only, and each child has a nurse assigned solely to them at all times." He opened the door and stepped inside. "We're monitoring him from down the hall, but Ginger is Nathan's nurse and will be in regularly to check on him."

They stepped inside, and Jessica saw her little boy, sleeping on the bed, with several monitors and wires around him and a nurse checking them and notating numbers from each machine on a clipboard in her hand. "Hello, I'm Ginger. I'll be taking care of Nathan today." She smiled pleasantly, then snapped her pen into place on the clipboard. "I'll be at the nurse's station, which is on the other side of the room, so I can be here immediately.

Just push this button to reach me." She indicated the red nurse button on the television remote.

Jessica moved to Nathan's side, took hold of his hand. She heard a deep, gravelly voice thank the nurse and then she turned to see it was Chad and that he still stood just inside the door, standing there, silently observing...his son.

"I'll be back in a few hours and will be in the hospital if anything changes," Dr. Aldredge said. "Ginger can reach me at all times."

Ginger glanced at Jessica, then Chad, then Nathan. "I'll leave you to stay with him," she said and left the room.

Jessica didn't know what to say to Chad, didn't know what he was thinking, what he was feeling. But she knew what the doctor said, that it may help Nathan to hear her voice. So she took his hand within hers and squeezed. "Hey, honey. Mommy is here. And I sure would love to see your pretty eyes now," she said. "Hey, guess what," she continued, her voice cracking from her throat closing in. "Nathan, Mommy has someone here you've been wanting to meet for a long time. Your daddy is here, baby, and he's looking forward to meeting you."

Chapter Twelve

Chad was mesmerized. His son. That beautiful boy in the hospital bed was his—his and Jessica's. He hadn't known this child, hadn't been there when she carried him in her womb, hadn't witnessed his birth. When Nathan's tiny hand first grasped a finger, it wasn't Chad's. And when he'd cried, Chad hadn't been there to hold him, comfort him.

He hadn't had a father…just like Chad hadn't had a father.

Jessica sat beside Nathan on one side of the bed. She was talking to him, soothing him, but Chad barely comprehended her words. He was too awestruck by the fact that this child was a part of him. Moving to the other side of the bed, Chad scooted the chair closer and took his hand. His little boy's hand. Nathan's hand.

Nathan. He hadn't named him, hadn't been there to help Jessica select it, but Nathan seemed to suit him somehow.

His hair was sandy brown, a little lighter than Chad's, but from what Chad remembered, it was about the same shade Chad's had been when he was a boy. His mouth was undeniably Jessica's, the full lower lip and tender cupid's bow forming the top.

Back when they were dating, Chad had always wondered what it would be like to have a child with Jess. He'd visualized her pregnant, putting a hand on her stomach and feeling the baby move inside. He'd done that, with Lainey, but he'd missed that with his son.

He'd missed a lot of things.

Jessica was still talking to Nathan, saying something about a Superman notebook. She wasn't done with her story, but Chad couldn't wait any longer. There were too many things he didn't know.

"When is his birthday?"

His question seemed to startle her, and Chad didn't mind that her eyes showed how guilty she felt that he had to ask. She deserved to feel guilty for keeping him from his son.

"February 16."

"So he'll be six…in a little over a week."

"A week from Wednesday," she said. "He was due on Valentine's Day, but he wasn't ready to come yet."

He could tell she'd told that a few times before, by the way her mouth inched up at the sides. And he could tell that she was hopeful that Chad would get over the fact that she'd kept him from his son. But she had no reason to be hopeful, not now anyway. The wound was too bitter and too reminiscent of a relationship filled with lies. But he had to talk to her now; that was the only way he could find out anything about his son. About the little boy he didn't know, hadn't met, who currently couldn't even tell Chad his name on his own.

"What's his name?" Chad asked. "His full name, I mean."

Another shadow of a smile passed over her lips. “Nathan Thomas Bowman.”

Chad’s heart leaped, but he didn’t let her see how much it meant that his son shared his middle name. Chad Thomas Martin and Nathan Thomas Bowman. If he’d have only known back then, Nathan’s last name would be Martin, too.

“I was going to tell you. I was always going to tell you,” she said.

Chad blinked several times, refusing to let her see how much her words affected him. Was she going to tell him? How could he know? She’d lied for all these years. What would keep her from lying now?

A knock sounded at the door, and then Bryant Bowman, a bandaged Anna and Chad’s mother, holding Lainey, walked in.

“Mom, are you okay?” Jess asked, staying by Nathan’s side but obviously concerned about the bandages on Anna’s head and face.

“Yes, dear. But how is Nathan? I finally convinced the nurses and doctors that I was all right, and then Nathan’s doctor told us we could come back and see him.”

“They don’t know what’s wrong,” Chad said. “There’s no physical or neurological reason that he shouldn’t wake up.”

“So, we just have to wait,” Bryant said.

Chad nodded. Then his attention turned to Lainey, reaching for him. He released Nathan’s hand momentarily to take his daughter.

“Dada,” she said, grinning broadly, then instinctively laying her head on his shoulder and tucking her thumb in her mouth. He curled one arm around her and took the other hand back to his son’s.

"Mom, how did you know to come?" he asked.

"Bryant called me and told me Jessica's little boy was hurt and that you were here," she said. "I thought I should come. I wasn't sure they'd let me bring Lainey back, but Bryant knew one of the nurses and said I could, for a few minutes." She looked at the bed, and her eyes widened, then her mouth opened slightly. "Chad?" she whispered.

Apparently the resemblance between himself and his son was even stronger than he realized. He looked at Jess, then her folks. "Can I have a moment alone with my mother…and my son?"

Jessica looked at him as though she couldn't believe he would ask her to leave.

"I've missed nearly six years," he said, his voice firm and low. "You can give me a few minutes now, can't you?"

Her shock at his tone, or perhaps his words, was obvious, and Chad felt a slight pang of regret at hurting her. But then he thought about how she'd hurt him, and he didn't stop her from exiting the room with her parents.

They had known. He had no doubt Bryant and Anna Bowman had known. All of them had known he had a son, and all of them had kept Nathan from him for six long years. And now his mother was also realizing what she'd missed because of Jessica.

Mae Martin moved closer to the bed, her mouth trembling and her tears dribbling down her cheeks. "Your son. He's yours," she whispered, marveling as she took in Nathan's features. "When—when did you find out?"

"Here, at the hospital," he said, unaware of how much time had passed since they'd left the small prayer room.

A prayer room where he'd issued a prayer for Jessica's son, without even realizing that Nathan was his son, too.

"He—" she gave a wobbly smile, moved to the chair where Jessica had sat and tenderly brushed her hand through Nathan's hair, then placed her hand upon his cheek "—he looks just like you did when you were little," she said, almost reverently. "Nathan," she whispered. "You are a very handsome young man."

Chad's heart squeezed in his chest. Those were the very words she'd said to him each time he got dressed up for a school function or for church, when the family had still attended church before his father left. He looked at his son, wondered how Nathan looked when he was all dressed up, and he wished he could see him that way. He wished he could see him open his eyes.

"His birthday is next Wednesday," Chad told her. "February 16. He'll be six."

She nodded, still tenderly stroking Nathan's cheek with her hand. "Born in the month for love," she said. "Now, isn't that special, Nathan?" She talked to him as though he was listening, and Chad hoped with all of his heart that he was.

"Mom?"

"Yes?" she asked, looking up from Nathan to peer through watery eyes at Chad. "What is it?"

"His middle name. It's Thomas."

Her smile pushed her cheeks toward her eyes, and the tears spilled over. "Your middle name and my daddy's name," she said, one handing covering her heart at the news. "I'm so—so glad Jessica did that."

Chad swallowed, glanced back at the little boy in the bed, at the way his mouth opened slackly and his eyes remained closed, with tiny fans of sandy lashes hiding their depths. Chad didn't even know the color of his eyes. "She kept him from me."

His mother continued looking at Nathan, as though she never wanted to stop, but her words were to Chad. "Why did she?"

He explained the timing, from what Jess had told him, and how she'd come to tell him the truth back then on the very night when he'd opened his scholarship letter.

His mother nodded through the whole story, then said, "It must have been a tough decision on her part, don't you think? Whether to tell you, knowing how you are, what a wonderful person you are, and that you'd have given up that scholarship to raise your child."

Chad was a little surprised at her train of thought. He'd have thought surely she'd have been just as upset as he was to learn she'd lost this time with her grandson. "She should have told me, Mom."

"Maybe if she could go back and do it again she would have."

Chad waited for her to continue, but she seemed lost in thought for a moment, and he wondered where her mind had headed, looking at her grandson in that bed.

"There are lots of things people would change if they could, but then, then you have to wonder what the true results would be if you made that change." She took her gaze from Nathan to Chad, and in that moment he knew exactly what she was thinking. If she could go back and change something, she could have chosen not to marry his father. But if she made that change, she wouldn't have Chad or Becky.

So she'd do it all again.

And if Jessica went back and told him the truth, he'd

have never left for Georgia and wouldn't have the beautiful little angel currently sleeping on his shoulder.

"You know, Chad, we're blessed that he's here." Her tears continued to flow, and she wiped her cheeks. "Jessica had more than those two options back then, you know, to tell you or to have Nathan on her own. And lots of girls would have taken another way out."

Knowing Jessica and her convictions, Chad hadn't even thought of that, that there would have been the option not to have the child at all or to have him and give him up for adoption.

His mother lifted Nathan's hand and kissed it, took her eyes back to her grandson. "He's your little boy. And I'm going to pray for him, to pray that I get to talk to him and meet him and love him the way I love Lainey."

Chad couldn't remember the last time he'd even heard his mother mention prayer.

"Chad," she said, her voice as tender as it'd been when she spoke to Nathan.

"Yes?"

"I know you're hurting, that it's hard to believe that a person you trusted so much and that you obviously love so much could have kept your son from you, but imagine how she's hurting now. Imagine how much she needs you now, to help her through this time. You are parents, the two of you, and you have a chance to be there for each other while Nathan needs you, both of you." She forced a smile, but her cheeks quivered with the effort, her emotions were so strong.

"I'm so disappointed with her right now," he said, thinking that disappointed was way too weak a word but not knowing a better one to describe his pain.

"I know she's hurt you, but don't—don't make her

go through this alone. It's so hard going through raising a child alone, and that's what she's been doing all this time, not because you left her, but because she was trying to do what was best for you. And I know what it's like to go through raising a child—two children—without someone there for you, without someone you can depend on, especially during the hard times. This is a hard time, and she's got to be scared that Nathan won't come through this okay. You can't turn your back on her now. Jessica needs you, and Nathan needs you, too."

Her words, straight from her heart, tore at his very soul.

"They're praying for him, out in the lobby. There's a big group from the church praying for him, and I'm going back out there, and I'm going to pray, too. I'm praying for Nathan, and I'm praying for you." She kissed Nathan's hand again, then stood and walked to Chad. "I'm sorry, Chad. I know that I haven't been the best example for you. I gave up relying on people, and I gave up on God years ago. What happened with you and Kate caused you to do the same, but I don't want you to go as long as I have before realizing that it isn't good to simply focus on who to blame. I saw them out there, praying together for Jessica's son—for *your* son—and I thought how amazing that must be to have someone you can trust to help you through the hard times."

He frowned. "That's the problem, Mom. How can I trust her now?"

"Oh, hon, I wasn't talking about trusting a person to get you through. I'd forgotten to trust in God, and seeing them out there, all together and calling on him, reminded me that He's there, even when others let me down." She reached for Lainey, and Chad stood, then transferred the beautiful sleeping girl from his arms to hers. "And Jessica can earn your trust again," she whispered. "But you need to give her a chance. And right now, you need to let her back in to be with her son, with your son. It's got to be killing her that you asked her to go. Trust me, I know."

A thick wave of guilt passed over him, and he nodded. "I'll go get her."

"And I'll go learn to pray again, for that precious little gift from God." She glanced one more time at the bed. "He'll be okay. I truly believe it, if we pray, surely, he'll be okay."

Chad was amazed at the transformation he'd just witnessed. His mother hadn't mentioned God, prayer or believing in God as long as he could remember, yet today, seeing her grandson and wanting him to be okay, that's exactly what she did. Deep down, she'd known who to turn to. God.

And deep down, Chad knew he'd done wrong by turning his back on Jessica, even if she'd hurt him. And he also knew who he needed to turn to now. But he wanted someone beside him when he did.

He wanted Jess.

Jessica cradled the cup of coffee within her hands as she ambled down the hallway with her parents. She ached inside, knowing Nathan was in that room and she wasn't there, but Chad was right; he deserved a few minutes alone with his son. She'd had six years with him, and—thanks to her—he'd had none.

"They're down here," her father said, guiding her and her mother down the hallway.

Jess had been so upset when the doctor brought them to Nathan's room that she couldn't remember the path back to the E.R. lobby. Evidently, her father did, because he continued as though he knew exactly where he was going, which was more than Jessica could say. She didn't know where she was going or what she was going to do, for that matter. What would she do if Nathan wasn't okay? And what would she do if Chad never forgave her?

A tall man wearing a baseball jersey similar to the one Chad had been wearing met them in the hall before they made it to the E.R. He looked familiar, his red hair peeking out from beneath the cap and his face a ruddy mass of freckles so dense that he appeared to have a tan.

"Jessica?" he asked. Then he moved closer and repeated, "Jessica. How is he? How's your little boy?"

She hadn't seen Mitch Gillespie in years, but that didn't matter. The friendship they'd shared was still right there, and his caring question proved it. "Still unconscious," she said and amazingly held back her tears with the words. "How did you know about him?" The question could have meant two things. One, how did Mitch Gillespie even know she had a son, and two, how did he know Nathan was here, hurt, in the hospital.

"I was with Chad when he got the message," Mitch said. He bit his lower lip, then asked, "So, Jess, is it true, what they're saying out there?" he indicated behind him, where she assumed the E.R. lobby was. "Is he Chad's?"

Jessica's shock must have been easily displayed, because Mitch quickly backtracked.

"I'm sorry, Jess. Small-town talk and all. I shouldn't

have said anything, but, well, I know how much that would mean to Chad, and I just wanted you to know that Jana and I are here for you, for both of you now."

Mitch had never been very good with tact, always managing to be brutally honest instead of thinking things through a bit before he blurted out whatever was on his mind. However, even though his first question had taken her off guard, the sentiment that he would be here for them during this tough time, touched her heart. "Thanks," she said. "That means a lot."

Mitch peered past her. "Where's Chad?"

"He's with Nathan," she said and again wished that she were there, too.

Mitch nodded. "You coming to the lobby? I can show you the way."

Her father had been leading, but she now noticed that he and her mother had stepped to the side while she had the rather uncomfortable conversation with her old friend. "We'd appreciate that," her dad said, and Jessica joined in step with him, Mitch and her mother to continue down the hall.

They rounded a corner, and she viewed the two large doors identifying the lobby. Mitch pushed a button on the wall and the doors swung open…revealing a lobby overflowing with people who appeared to all be waiting for her.

"How is he? How's Nathan? What did the doctor say?" The questions came quickly, and Jessica did her best to answer. Then she noticed Chad's mother, sitting in a corner chair with Lainey, still sleeping, on her shoulder. Jess walked to her, sat beside her.

"I'm praying for him, for Nathan," Mae said, her hand

stroking Lainey's soft hair as she spoke. "And for you and for Chad."

"I'm sorry," Jess said, "for keeping him from you."

Mae blinked a couple of times, her eyes soft and warm. "Oh, honey, you had some tough decisions to make, and I'm not sure what I'd have done in your shoes. But you've given me a grandson, and I'll always be grateful for that. And Chad will come around, dear. He's just, well, he's just been hurt a lot. It's tough to get over something like that. But I'm praying for him." She smiled thoughtfully. "Been a long time since I've talked to God, and it feels pretty good."

Trying not to disturb Lainey, Jessica eased toward Mae and gently hugged her. "Thank you." She turned to see several guys clad in baseball jerseys all gathered together on one side of the lobby with Mitch conveying Nathan's current condition—and knowing Mitch, probably also conveying the fact that their buddy was a father. She watched for a shocked reaction but only noticed smiles, and then she saw the group gather in a circle and bow their heads. For their son. The scene touched her heart immensely.

Brother Henry and his wife were speaking to Jessica's parents, and several other members of the church were gathered around, their heads bowed and hands joined in prayer for Nathan. Hannah, wearing the same pink-and-green hat she'd worn Wednesday night, was in the center of a group of women and appeared to be leading the prayer. Her T-shirt and jeans didn't go with the hat, and Jess had the realization that Nathan's teacher, who'd matched from her hat to her shoes Wednesday night, had left her house in a rush to get here. Again, her heart was touched.

"Jessica," Brother Henry's voice stole her attention from the scene. "We'd like to have everyone pray together while you're here, before you go back to Nathan's room again, if that's okay with you."

"Yes, please," she said, standing.

Brother Henry gathered all of the small groups together to form one large circle. "Let's join hands," he said, and they did, Jessica wrapping an arm around Chad's mother, since her arms were filled with her granddaughter.

Jessica had already bowed her head when she felt another arm settle over hers to cradle Chad's mom, and she thought she knew who it was, even before she glanced up to see Chad. His hand gently squeezed her forearm, and he looked directly at her.

"I'm sorry," he whispered.

"I am, too."

Jessica saw wet drops fall from his mother's bowed head to the floor, and then she heard Brother Henry's prayer begin, and she bowed her head once more.

"Dear Father, we know that with You all things are possible, and we know that You are here with us, and that You are with Nathan. Help him, God. Help him to heal and to open his eyes to be with us again, to be with his mama and his daddy and everyone here who loves him so much. And watch over his parents, Lord, and his grandparents. Help them to be there for each other and to be strong in each other and in You as they face this difficult time. In Jesus' blessed holy name, amen."

Jessica's eyes were wet, her heart touched by the heartfelt prayer, one that included Nathan's parents without being judgmental that one of those parents was just identified to the group today. Obviously, they all knew, but no one cared about the where or when or how that Chad Martin had learned he was Nathan's father; they simply cared about Nathan. And the man who'd kissed his mother's cheek, gently patted his daughter's back and was now taking Jessica's hand not only cared about his son but also appeared to still care about her, in spite of her dishonesty.

"Let's go back to our son," he said, leading her from the group and back to the hall. Then, to Brother Henry and Jessica's father, he said, "We'll let you know if anything changes. Please keep praying."

They both promised they would, and then Chad and Jessica quickly made their way back to Nathan's room.

"You forgive me," she said, breathlessly due to their pace.

He stopped just shy of Nathan's door. "I do, and I shouldn't have been so cold earlier, Jess. I was hurt, and I handled it wrong. It's not going to be easy living with me while I attempt to learn to trust again, but I'm hoping you're willing to try. Because I want to be with you, and I want us together. You, me, Lainey and Nathan. And he needs us now, together. He'll need us always, together."

"If I could change what I did back then..."

He shook his head. "God had a plan, and I'm not going to mess with that. And I pray that His plan will have Nathan waking up soon."

She nodded. "I pray that, too."

Chad pushed open the door, and the two of them moved to the bed and together took Nathan's hands.

"Hey, honey, it's Mom," she said. "We're here. Me, and your daddy. We're both here. And you've been waiting so long to meet him, Nathan. Don't you want to open your eyes and see him? You look a lot alike, you and your dad." She looked at Chad, and her heart melted at the unhidden love displayed in those exquisite eyes—love for her and love for their son.

He gave her an easy smile, then took a hand to Nathan's head and gently ruffled his hair. "Hey, buddy," he said. "Listen, I need you to wake up—for me, Daddy." His smile broadened with the endearing term, and tears shone in his eyes. "Because I've got big plans for us, and you can't be a part of them if you're sleeping. We're going to go to the park and feed the ducks. And then we'll ride bicycles. Do you like riding bicycles?"

"He's wanting to learn how to ride without the training wheels," Jess said. "But I'm not that great a teacher, and he kind of ended up in a holly bush the last time we tried."

Chad grinned. "Okay, Dad promises to take over with the bicycle lessons. Is that why you're sleeping so hard, because you're afraid Mom will send you into another holly bush?"

Jessica's heart warmed at the way Chad eased into the role of father, even when he hadn't officially met his son. She recalled Nathan's words after Brother Henry's lesson about daddies and knew that they were true. He really was "gonna love him."

But first he needed to wake up.

And Chad was determined to help that happen. "How about fishing? Has Mom taken you fishing yet? Because I know a great spot on the Coosa where the crappie always bite. We'll catch them and bring them home for Mom to clean and cook."

Jessica vehemently shook her head at that.

"Or not," he said, a hint of laughter in his tone. "And

what else would you like to do with me? Because we'll do whatever you want as soon as you wake up," he said.

"He wants to play baseball," Jessica said. "When we've talked about you before, when we talked about when he'd meet his daddy, Nathan said he wanted to play baseball with you…and eat ice cream."

Chad blinked, and she noticed his lashes were spiked with tears. "He was always planning to meet me."

"I was going to make sure it happened. I just didn't know when it would be."

A couple more blinks, then Chad leaned over Nathan and kissed his forehead. "Come on, slugger, let's wake up and go play some baseball." He raised up and looked at his son, and then he gasped, seeing the same thing as Jessica…a very slight, nearly imperceptible flutter of Nathan's lashes.

"Chad?" she questioned.

"Nathan," Chad said. "Nathan, are you going to go play baseball with me? Come on, baby. Open your eyes."

"We'll go get that Superman notebook you've been wanting," Jess said. "And the pencils," she said, willing those eyes to move again. *God, help him come back to us, please.*

"Hey, Nathan," Chad said. "Daddy can't wait to meet you and eat ice cream and play baseball and do everything you want."

Again, Nathan's eyes twitched, and then, while Jessica squeezed Chad's hand, they opened.

"Nathan!" she exclaimed, part yell, part laugh. "Oh, Nathan, Mommy missed you so much!"

Nathan's smile was a little slow getting started, but

then it eased customarily into his cheeks. "Missed you," he said, his voice a rough croak.

Jess laughed again and then said, "Nathan, there's someone here..."

She didn't get to finish. Nathan had already turned his attention to the man beside her, and his eyes squinted a little as he looked at Chad then grinned.

"You," he said, then licked his lips and tried again. "You're Daddy."

Chapter Thirteen

Chad had planned the perfect outing for Nathan's first full day out of the house. It'd been a week since the accident, and his follow-up visit to Dr. Aldredge yesterday went well. All in all, Nathan had ended up just fine, and the best way the doctor knew how to describe what had happened was that Nathan's body just needed a little more time to heal before he was ready to tackle the world again.

But Chad had another idea. He agreed with Jessica, her parents and his mother that God's plan included Nathan resting for a while so he and Jessica could deal with the past and plan for their future with Nathan and Lainey.

They'd started that future this week, spending time together each day letting Nathan and Lainey get to know each other and slowly getting Nathan back into full swing. Oh, he'd been ready to go full blast by Tuesday, not understanding why he couldn't go back to school yet. But Jessica wasn't budging from the doctor's orders. He'd gone back yesterday.

However, she did cave to every Superman desire,

which included not only the notebook and pencils he'd mentioned in the hospital but also pajamas, an oversize coloring book…and a real red cape. She'd found the cape at a party supply store and surprised him with it last night, and when she and Chad tucked him into bed at her parents' house, he'd still been wearing it.

Chad grinned. They'd made some memories this week. No, he couldn't make up every day that he'd missed with his son, but he could sure make certain that their time together now was well spent.

"So, when's the guest of honor getting here?" Mitch called from the dugout.

"They'll be here soon," Chad said and saw Jessica's car pulling in to the lot. "Here they are."

She had her hair pulled up in a ponytail and tucked through the back of a red baseball cap, and she wore a white baseball shirt with red sleeves, along with red cropped pants and white tennis shoes. Chad smiled as Nathan climbed out of the backseat. He was dressed in the jersey Chad had purchased yesterday, the one that matched his mom's…and his dad's. His red baseball cap was the fitted kind, not because he actually needed a fitted cap but because that's the kind his daddy wore, and he wanted to "look just like Dad."

Chad beamed.

Then Jessica leaned into the car, unhooked Lainey from her car seat and then propped her on her hip. Lainey, like the remainder of the group, wore a tiny white shirt with red sleeves and even had a baseball cap, trimmed in white eyelet lace. Chad and Jess had found the outfit last night, and they simply couldn't resist.

"Jana's gonna love you," Mitch said in his ear. "Because this picture is making me want kids."

The picture was perfect, Chad had to admit.

Nathan bounded ahead, with Jessica attempting to slow him down.

"Take it easy!" she yelled, then looked helplessly at Chad. "Don't let him overdo it."

"Hey, Daddy!" Nathan said, his arms outstretched and his giggle contagious as he ran into Chad's arms.

"I got you something," Chad said, kissing Nathan's cheek and carrying him into the dugout, where a small leather baseball glove, its seams a little tattered and worn, rested on the bench.

Nathan spotted it immediately, moved to pick it up and slipped it on his hand. "Cool!" Then he turned it and saw the black marking on the side. His mouth quirked to the side. "Hey, that's not my name."

"No, it's mine," Chad said. "That was my first glove, and now it's yours." He touched his hand to the soft leather. "It's broken in already, so it'll be easier for you to catch balls."

Nathan grinned, still marveling at the glove. "That's your name," he said, pointing to the messy black scribble.

Chad nodded and even recalled the day he'd taken that fat black marker and used it to identify his most prized possession. "Yep, it says Chad Martin."

Nathan looked away from Chad and to Jess, walking toward the bleachers with Lainey on her hip and playing with Jessica's ponytail. "Mom!" he called.

"Yes, honey, what is it?"

"Dad's glove says Chad Martin," he said.

"I know, but it's your glove now. And I bet Daddy will let you put your name on it, too."

"Not yet, though. I'll wait," Nathan said softly.

"Why is that?" Chad asked.

"'Cause Mommy said one day my name might be like yours," Nathan said matter-of-factly, rubbing his small fingers over the black letters on the leather. Then he looked up and squinted at Chad. "I might be Nathan Martin," he said. "One day."

Chad looked toward Jessica, but she was busying herself trying to find Lainey's beloved pappy in the diaper bag.

"I'm sure it's in here somewhere," she was saying while Lainey whimpered because her request wasn't being met as quickly as she wanted.

Chad smiled, crouched down in front of his son. "Nathan, this is going to be our special secret. Can you keep a secret?"

Nathan wrinkled up his nose and squished his mouth tight. Then he sighed. "Not very good," he said.

Mitch snickered from where he leaned against the chain link forming the dugout, and Chad laughed. He touched Nathan's nose. "All right then, I'll wait and tell you later, so it won't be so hard on you."

"'K," Nathan said, smiling and sliding his hand in and out of the glove. "Daddy?"

Chad would never get tired of hearing that. "Yes?"

"This is your team, right?"

"Right."

"What's the name of it?" Nathan asked.

"The name of my team?"

Nathan bobbed his head. "Yeah, Anson's team is the Rangers, but he don't know if he'll be the Rangers again this year."

"Our team is just plain ol' Claremont," Mitch said, smiling at Nathan. "Not as exciting as Rangers, huh?"

"That's okay," Nathan said.

"Who is Anson?" Chad asked.

"One of the boys at school. My friend," Nathan clarified. "His daddy is his coach."

"Is he now?" Chad asked and was very glad Jess had informed him of Nathan's baseball plans, because he'd have never thought to check into the T-ball sign-ups otherwise. And he'd sure never have signed up to take on a team at next weekend's enrollment day. "Well, isn't that a coincidence?"

Nathan looked up. "What?"

"That his daddy is coaching his team and that your daddy will be coaching yours. We're the Cardinals, though. Think that'll be cool enough?"

Nathan's squeal of delight caused Jessica to stand from the bleachers.

"Everything okay?" she yelled. "Is he all right?"

"Dad's going to be my coach! And we're the Cardinals!"

She laughed. "I was wondering when he'd tell you about that. Pretty cool, huh?"

"Definitely!" Nathan said, his smile broad and wide. Then he asked, "Was that the secret?"

Chad saw Jessica's head tilt to the side, and he gave her a wink. "That was one secret, but I may just have another one soon."

"Cool," Nathan said.

"So, you gonna figure out how to use that glove, or are you going to sit in the dugout?" Mitch asked Nathan. The other guys on the team had been fielding the entire time he, Mitch and Nathan were chatting, but they didn't seem to mind that their teammates were taking their time. They were all as thrilled with Nathan's presence as Chad was, nearly. Besides, this practice wasn't exactly on the schedule. Chad had asked them to get together today for the sole purpose of entertaining his son. And none of them minded at all.

Nathan was intent on learning as much as possible, taking turns at each position in the field with one of Chad's friends by his side at each rotation. The guys loved it, and Nathan definitely enjoyed practicing with the "big guys." Every now and then, after he'd caught a ball or made a throw, he'd yell at his mom to see if Lainey saw him. Jessica was extra careful that even if Lainey was paying more attention to her pappy or her thumb than the game at least she was looking in Nathan's direction and giving the impression of rooting for her big brother.

That seemed to be enough for Nathan. And it was perfect for Chad, who knew that only one thing would make his life more complete.

He planned to take care of that soon, by tomorrow, if his "secret" worked out right.

Jessica wore a white dress with a red belt and red heels to church Sunday morning. It wasn't a usual type of outfit for her, but Valentine's Day was nearly here, and she was feeling the sentiment of the holiday completely, more than she had in a long time. In six years.

She smiled as she and her parents pulled into the church parking lot and parked beside Chad's BMW. He'd told Nathan that they would all go to church together today, and then he'd promised Jess that they would all go to church together always.

The past weeks had been crammed with emotions, and not all of them good, but the outcome was worth the journey. And the fact that it brought them here, to church together, with their son, really made it all worthwhile. She saw Chad, standing near the building with Lainey on his hip and his mother by his side.

Jessica couldn't remember the last time she'd seen Mae at church, but Chad's mother looked truly happy to be here. She saw them and smiled brightly. "There's our little man," she said as Nathan approached.

Nathan ran to her and hugged her knees. "Hey, Miss Mae," he said.

Chad smirked. For some reason, his mother's name had caught on with Nathan, and although Chad tried to get him to go with MeMaw, or Mimi, or Grandma, or some other traditional term after he realized that she was his grandmother, Nathan had continued calling her "Miss Mae." And what was even funnier was how much she loved it.

She squeezed Nathan in return and laughed when he took her hand and started leading her toward the church steps. "Come on, I'll show you where my class is, and you can meet Ms. Hannah."

"Sounds wonderful," she said, winking at Chad and Jessica as she allowed her grandson to lead her inside.

Brother Henry was at the top of the stairs, and he eyed Nathan. "You going to earn that peppermint today?" he asked.

"Of course!" Nathan said, grinning.

"Nice to see you here, Mae," he said, shaking her free hand before Nathan jerked her other one to bring her into the lobby.

"It's wonderful to be here," she said, then continued inside.

Chad wrapped an arm around Jessica, and they followed her parents up the stairs to enter the church.

"Having a better weekend than last weekend, I see," Brother Henry said.

Jessica nodded, "Much better. And thank you so much for everything last week. For all of the prayers, and for being there at the hospital with us."

"I wouldn't have been anywhere else," Brother Henry said. "And we received your thank-you note to the church. It's printed in today's bulletin." Then he seemed to think of something and said, "We haven't put the bulletin out yet. I'll get someone to pass them out shortly, though."

"That's fine," Jess said. "I appreciate you printing the note. It did mean the world to me that all of you came and prayed for my—for our—son."

Chad thanked him as well, and they entered the auditorium for the adult Bible study. As usual, Brother Henry let the adults with young children out early to go pick up their children from class. Chad and Jessica stood to go get Lainey and Nathan.

Jessica nodded toward the first hallway, the one with the nursery and toddler classes. "I'll go get Lainey."

Chad smiled, obviously knowing that she was trying once again to give him something he hadn't had before, the chance to pick up his son from Bible class. "Thanks."

Lainey was holding a cloth book that had a picture of a manger on the front. Seeing Jessica, she pointed to the little manger, pulled her pacifier from her mouth and said, "Baby."

"That's right," Jess said. "Baby Jesus."

Lainey displayed all of her tiny teeth in a big smile,

then popped her "pappy" back in her mouth and reached for Jess.

"Come on, we'll go see Daddy and Nathan in big church," Jess said, carrying her back to the auditorium, where her parents, Mae, Chad and Nathan were already seated on a pew. She sat beside Chad and let Lainey climb into his lap. Then she noticed Nathan, his hand covering his mouth while he giggled.

He looked…guilty.

"What are you up to?" she asked, and he laughed even harder.

Chad, she also noticed, looked equally blameworthy.

And, now that she examined them, so did her father, her mother and even Mae. Everyone smiling at her as though she had some kind of ugly stain on her dress… or something.

"What am I missing?" She looked down, saw nothing out of sorts.

"You'll see," Nathan said, and Chad frowned at him. Not a real frown, but one that said he expected him to hold it together. Or at least keep whatever it was he knew—that everyone on the pew knew—to himself.

Nathan slapped both hands over his mouth now, his laughter was muffled by the obstruction.

"Okay, you're worrying me," Jess said, which caused Nathan to giggle even more, until he actually snorted.

"Chad, what did you say to him?"

Brother Henry cleared his throat at the pulpit, and Jessica attempted to turn her attention away from her perplexing family.

She wondered why Brother Henry was doing the announcements. Typically he only did that when they were having a guest speaker, and she hadn't noticed a guest speaker in the bulletin today. Then again, she hadn't been able to review the bulletin, since Brother Henry had said it wasn't out when they arrived.

Jessica glanced at the song racks on the back of the pew in front of them but didn't see a bulletin. Sighing, she tuned out Nathan's continued muffled laughter and focused on listening to Brother Henry. Then she saw the teenage boys stand at the front of the building with baskets filled with bulletins in their arms. Brother Henry mentioned that they had a special announcement today and that it was imprinted on the front page of the bulletin.

She supposed the announcement had to do with whoever was speaking, and she peered around the heads in front of them to try to see who was sitting in the traditional preacher's spot on the front row. Unfortunately, they'd sat on the next to last row, probably in case Lainey had to go out before church was done, so there were lots of heads to see around.

But as she tried to see the front of the building, Jessica noticed the strangest thing. One by one, row by row, the people in the auditorium turned around and appeared to be looking…at her.

As the bulletins continued making their way from row to row, the people in each row turned.

"You must have written a really amazing thank you note," Chad said.

Jessica felt her cheeks heating. She had written a nice note, but she didn't understand this response to it. Everyone peered at her, stared at her, and Nathan's giggles were getting uncontrollable. She looked at him and quietly tried to shush him, which, naturally, made him worse.

"Chad? Something's not right," she whispered.

"Oh, I think it is," he said, not making sense at all.

Finally the teens reached the ends of her pew, and then she saw them look at each other and shake their heads, then skip their pew and go to the one behind them.

Jessica wasn't in the habit of turning around and gawking in church, but she did glance over her shoulder, then tried to motion to the boy nearest her end that she wanted a bulletin, too.

When he seemed not to see her, which she didn't think possible, she looked toward the teen at the other end and saw Chad give him a nod. Then the boy passed the basket to her father, who slowly passed it to her mother, then Mae, then Nathan, then Chad…and finally to Jessica. She took a copy, then handed the basket to the boy on her end, who was now looking directly at her.

And then it hit her. The whole church, even Brother Henry at the pulpit—was silent. And the whole church, even Brother Henry at the pulpit—was watching her.

She glanced at the paper in her hand and saw the "special announcement" on the front page.

Mr. and Mrs. Bryant Bowman and Ms. Mae Martin request your presence this Wednesday, Valentine's Day, at the Claremont Christian Church as Jessica Diane Bowman and Chad Thomas Martin exchange their vows and begin their new life together at 4:00 p.m. A reception will follow at Hydrangea Park amid the Valentine's light display.

And beneath the "announcement" in a whimsical font that she was certain her groom had selected, a single line was printed.

This is, of course, assuming she said yes.

The whole church waited. Nathan giggled. And Chad pulled a small box from his pocket. "Just say yes," he said, reminding her of that night when he'd asked her to have a relationship with him, after that first coffee shop date. Now he was asking her to have a lifetime with him—a lifetime with him and Nathan and Lainey.

"Yes."

Epilogue

Merely a few weeks ago when she first ran into Chad that cool crisp night on the Stockville campus, Jessica had experienced that bizarre sensation of feeling as though she was merely watching life occur around her, when an individual wasn't actually participating in the event but an onlooker, observing the activity and wondering how the scene would play out. She supposed it was because the instance was so close to a "dream come true" feeling.

Then she'd thought the feeling unique, probably something she wouldn't experience again.

She'd been wrong.

Because right now, stepping into the church of her youth with her Daddy by her side, her friends and family turning and looking at her with broad smiles of approval on their faces, Jessica definitely know the sensation of a dream come true.

But it wasn't the church building, or her father by her side, or all of the friends and family that made this moment so right. It was the reason that they were all here, an event that merely months ago she'd have believed would only ever happen in her dreams.

She was marrying Chad Martin, the love of her life and the father of her precious son, in front of God and—from the look of the packed church—in front of the majority of Claremont.

Before they took the first step down the aisle, her father leaned toward her and kissed her cheek. Then he whispered, "I remember standing at the front of the church and seeing your Mom in that dress."

Jessica glanced down at the dress she'd always planned to wear on her wedding day, the creamy satin shimmering and the tiny pearls that Jessica's grandmother had sewn to the bodice glistening in the church light. "I'm so glad Mom saved it for me. It makes everything perfect."

He squeezed her hand and smiled. "That dress is special," he said, emotion filling every word, "but I'd say what makes this day perfect is the trio waiting for you at the end of the aisle."

Jessica glanced toward the front of the church, where Brother Henry held his Bible close to his heart and smiled, and where the trio her father mentioned waited. Lainey sat on the steps near Brother Henry's feet, her basket of flower petals beside her and her attention on her big brother. She looked up toward Nathan and gave him a full grin, then handed him a couple of red rose petals. Nathan took the petals and smiled. Then he noticed Jessica, looked up at his Daddy and pointed to his mom.

"Dad, look! Mom looks great!" His exclamation caused a few chuckles to ripple through the guests and made Jessica laugh.

But Nathan didn't have anything to worry about. Chad hadn't taken his eyes off of her since she entered the auditorium, and Jessica couldn't think of a time when she'd ever felt more loved.

While the wedding march played, Jessica and her father made their way to the front and to her waiting family. Lainey immediately reached for Jessica's bouquet, and Jessica smiled as she handed it to her toddler.

"Tank oo," Lainey said, and Nathan sniggered.

Then Brother Henry conducted a short ceremony, and then finally pronounced that they were now Mr. and Mrs. Chad Thomas Martin and informed Chad that he could kiss his bride.

Chad pulled her close, his green-gold eyes glistening a bit at the emotion obviously tugging at his heart. "Mrs. Martin," he whispered, "You've just made me the happiest man in the world." Then he brought his lips to hers and kissed her softly, sweetly…until Nathan giggled and they both looked at their son, his hand over his mouth, and smiled. Then Chad scooped Nathan into his arms and kissed his cheek, and Jess took Lainey in hers and did the same.

"What a beautiful celebration for Valentine's Day," Brother Henry said from behind them. He grinned. "And now, ladies and gentlemen, I can pronounce the Martin family."

The entire crowd broke out into cheers and applause, while Chad, Jessica, Nathan and Lainey—the Martin family—officially began their life together.

Two days later, Nathan celebrated his sixth birthday, with his Mommy, Daddy, MeMaw, Granddaddy, Miss Mae and Lainey surrounding him, along with his new

Uncle Rob and Aunt Becky, who'd flown in from Alaska for the wedding.

Jessica admired the beauty of her family and the amazing blessings she'd received in the past year. "It doesn't get any more perfect than this."

Nathan laughed. "Yes, it does." He didn't explain, but obviously her little man knew what he was talking about. Because after his party, they all loaded up in their cars and headed to the local Little League sign-ups, where his daddy became the new coach for the Cardinals T-ball team and where Nathan found out he would be wearing the number 1 jersey. Then, after donning his new jersey and cap, they got in their car again and headed out for ice cream.

He licked the side of his chocolate ice cream cone and then grinned at his new, big family. "Now," he told his mom, "it doesn't get any more perfect than this!"

Jessica laughed, and Chad wrapped an arm around her pulling her close to his side.

"Nathan," he said. "You're exactly right."

* * * * *

Dear Reader,

Her Valentine Family touched my heart because it focuses on issues that everyone deals with in a lifetime—forgiveness and trust. Jessica withholds the truth from someone she loves because she believes she is protecting him, but she doesn't realize the impact of keeping her secret. Chad has been betrayed in the past—not only by his first wife but by his father. Those facts play a huge part in Chad's relationship with God and in his ability to forgive. Forgiving isn't always easy, but all things are possible with God, as Chad and Jessica learn in *Her Valentine Family.*

My website—www.reneeandrews.com—includes an alternate beginning for the novel and a deleted scene that didn't make the final cut but will give you the background on what Jessica went through when she made that difficult decision to move to Tennessee.

And if you have prayer requests, there's a place to let me know on my site. I will lift your request up to the Lord in prayer. I love to hear from readers, so please write to me at renee@reneeandrews.com.

Blessings in Christ,

Renee Andrews

QUESTIONS FOR DISCUSSION

1. Jessica left her parents and the only home she'd ever known when she was just sixteen and pregnant. Have you ever had to leave home? How did you deal with it?

2. After learning about Chad's scholarship, Jessica thought the right thing to do was to leave him and keep the truth of their child a secret until his situation was better. Is it ever right to withhold the truth? Is withholding the truth the same as telling a lie?

3. Chad believes that he can no longer trust anyone with his heart. What Bible Scripture would you recommend to someone with trust issues?

4. Jessica's concern for Nathan after receiving the phone call from his teacher consumed her thoughts so much that she couldn't concentrate on her class. Have you ever been worried that something was wrong with a child? How did you handle that concern?

5. A blending of families can sometimes be difficult on children. Most individuals have experienced some form of family blending, whether in their immediate or extended family. How did Chad and Jessica use the difference in Nathan and Lainey's ages as an advantage for how they helped Nathan accept his new sister? What could a family do if the children were older when their families join?

6. Chad had a difficult time trusting. After Kate betrayed his trust so completely, he couldn't consider trusting her again. However, Jessica also betrayed his trust, yet he found a way to forgive her for keeping her secret. What was different about the two situations that caused Chad to be able to forgive Jess?

7. Jessica described her return to her home church as feeling like the prodigal son. Have you ever experienced that feeling? Were you welcomed with open arms, like the way Brother Henry welcomed Jessica back? Or were you met with resistance, like those whispering in the lobby?

8. Why do you think Mae found it so easy to relate to Jessica? How did her past affect her interpretation?

9. Jessica and Chad were both touched by the gathering of people in the emergency room to pray for their son. How much does it mean to know others are praying for you in times of need?

10. In researching this book, I learned from doctors who believe patients can hear when they are unconscious, and I also learned from doctors who believed they couldn't. There have been studies regarding both options. What do you think? Do you have any personal reason to feel that way?

Love Inspired®

TITLES AVAILABLE NEXT MONTH

Available February 22, 2011

A PLACE TO BELONG
Redemption River
Linda Goodnight

MENDING HER HEART
Judy Baer

A DAD OF HIS OWN
Dreams Come True
Gail Gaymer Martin

A COLORADO MATCH
Deb Kastner

IN A DOCTOR'S ARMS
Lisa Mondello

FAMILY TO THE RESCUE
Moonlight Cove
Lissa Manley

LICNM0211